PONY BOYS

PONY BOYS

RICHARD PROSCH

FIVE STAR
A part of Gale, a Cengage Company

LIBRARY OF CONGRESS CATALOGING-IN-PUBLICATION DATA

Names: Prosch, Richard, author.
Title: Pony boys / Richard Prosch.
Description: First edition. | Waterville, Maine : Five Star, a part of Gale, a Cengage Company, [2022] | Identifiers: LCCN 2022018056 | ISBN 9781432899103 (hardcover)
Subjects: LCSH: Middleton, Doc, 1851–1913—Fiction. | BISAC: FICTION / Historical / General | FICTION / Westerns | LCGFT: Historical fiction | Western fiction | Novels.
Classification: LCC PS3616.R656 P66 2022 | DDC 813/.6—dc23/eng/20220426
LC record available at https://lccn.loc.gov/2022018056

First Edition. First Printing: December 2022
Find us on Facebook—https://www.facebook.com/FiveStarCengage
Visit our website—http://www.gale.cengage.com/fivestar
Contact Five Star Publishing at FiveStar@cengage.com

Printed in Mexico
Print Number: 1 Print Year: 2023

For Wyatt, who rode with me

CHAPTER ONE

In 1877 I was fourteen years old, and I'd left my northern Nebraska home for a freight load of reasons, half of which I can hardly recall and the other half don't matter, except for one and she was my mother, and she don't matter a whole hell of a lot either.

But enough about her.

What do you know but one day I found myself without food or fortune in a dirty livery stable outside Julesburg, pitching rocks into the street. Not a thing more to do but get mixed up in whatever nonsense galloped my way.

I wasn't looking for work, but I'll tell you what—I was looking.

When the man with the gold tooth and long bird's-nest beard said his name was Jim Cherry, dealer in stock, and he'd pay me five dollars to keep my mouth shut, I couldn't help but follow after him in the barn.

Heck, I knew keeping quiet was the neighborly thing to do.

In the unorganized territories west, it was the only smart thing.

He told me he had a plan to traipse out of there with a string of horses, past a line of corral hands, right under the nose of the stable manager, slick as sheep dip, and "How-do-you-do? My name is Jim Cherry."

Naturally, the horses didn't belong to Jim.

If I wanted, he said I could tag along the trail with him a

ways. But only if I helped him liberate the horses and keep quiet about it afterwards.

I asked for my money.

Jim handed me the five, and I told him my name was August John.

He said "Oh, really?" and raised his eyebrows.

"You probably heard of me."

"No. I never have."

Which sort of perturbed me.

My Christian name is John Augustus, but most folks called me Gus. I guess they still do. When the papers started writing about the Niobrara River horse thieves and Chief Little Wound's missing nags, when they started calling some of us a rowdy bunch of owlhoots and rascals—and sometimes worse—a smart aleck reporter referred to me as *August John.*

Wouldn't you know, the moniker stuck?

Hard to believe Jim didn't read the papers.

But we worked together, the two of us, a while, getting them critters ready to go, a blood bay and a strawberry roan and a flaxen chestnut mare like I'd never seen before. She was all of spring bundled up and unleashed on the range, all this fresh life and energy sparking under a clean, well-groomed hide.

Jim had this round plug of tobacco packed up like an orange stuck in his shirt pocket. He pulled it out and took a bite like an apple.

Then he tossed it over to me. I took a bite, tossed it back. He flung it over again.

We went along in such a way, hurling the wad of 'baccy back and forth, just playing catch like we had all the time in the world.

I'll never forget looking out the stable doors opening onto the prairie and the trail leading off to the east. The butterflies were thick on the frontier and the bluestem had gone to seed, and when the forever wind of the high plains blew, it made waves in the grass, sweeping the bugs up into cyclone spirals mid-flight.

It was quite the sight, those determined butterflies bucking the breeze. I knew how they felt.

Jim had his own dun gelding, and I picked out a similar-colored mare I'd taken a shine to.

I didn't know who she belonged to, but I figured her owner likely had plenty of money and more than one horse.

Remember the story of Robin Hood? It's the way things were with me.

Jim wasn't making much in the way of conversation, but seeing as we were engaged in Robin Hood–type activities, I started talking about Doc Middleton, the famous horse thief who haunted the Niobrara country.

I said, "The sumbuck was a drover up from Texas on the Chisholm Trail. 'Tis how I understand it."

"I wouldn't know," said Jim, stroking his beard, thoughtful-like.

"Went to work for that big cattle outfit outside of North Platte—you heard of them ain't you? Shoot, everybody's heard of them. Why am I even asking?"

The day was drowsy drunk with specks of dust floating in the sunbeams and clouds of flies buzzing around the manure pile outside the back doors. I felt like a real bigshot talking real-world things—cattle outfits and hands on the Chisholm.

Me and Jim were getting along pretty well when I said, "Yeah, I sure wouldn't mind meeting up with ol' Doc one day."

Jim smiled real sheepish then, and here I was running on at the piehole, so wonderfully boneheaded. It's the curse of youth. I have no other excuse.

My blond hair fell curly on my shoulders back then—like General Custer. And as with that old personage of yore, my ego sometimes left the gate without a saddle.

I didn't figure on growing a beard, though.

"Tell ya one thing," I told Jim, "old Doc Middleton wouldn't worry me none if I ever did meet him. He's one varmint I wouldn't be scared to look dead in the eye."

When Jim laughed it was real quiet, meaning you honestly couldn't hear him at all, just a sort of brushing of cottonwood leaves in the wind, but you knew he was getting a kick out of something because his shoulders where pumping up and down, shrugging with mirth.

I was encouraged by his response, and when one of the local hands sauntered through, I grabbed a pitchfork to move a few horse apples and kept talking.

Jim and me both nodded at the cowpoke, and he moved along without giving us a second thought. I leaned on my fork.

"They say Doc killed a man out in a Sidney dance hall. He's wanted for the murder this very day."

I knew the story well.

"Everybody's heard about Soldier-boy Keefe and how he got shot up. Heard he gave Doc two hard blows. Sent him reeling into the bar and onto the floor but kept coming at him. Doc was simply defending himself." I couldn't help but embellish the tale some. "Still and all, after the killing, Middleton snuck out of town on the Deadwood Stage to Fort Robinson like a yellow-bellied polecat."

By now Jim was howling with laughter and clutching his stomach with both hands.

"It is funny to imagine," I said. But maybe not *so* funny.

Jim said, "I don't have to imagine it. I lived it. I am Doc Middleton," and he pulled out his big Smith & Wesson Model 3 .44 revolver and pointed it at the bridge of my nose.

This is the kind of turn of events what plagued much of my early life.

"A fine how-de-do," I said, looking down the barrel of Doc's gun.

It was a nice weapon. Not as nice as the Peacemaker he got later from Trudy, or the one he died with, which they hung up in O'Neill for near twenty years—but damn neared as purty.

I stomped my floppy boots around in a circle. "I'm here helping you out, and now you're fixing to shoot me."

"You promised to keep your mouth shut," Doc said. "It's pretty clear you won't do that."

"I was just passing the time," I countered. "Until some of these cowboys and hired hands move out."

He waved the barrel of the .44 around in a circle, the late afternoon sun glinting off his big damn gold tooth. "S'pect you're a little bit more scared of ol' Doc now, ain'tcha?"

"S'pect it's more like irritation."

Then came more laughing and stroking of the beard. Thing about Doc's beard—he grew it long, down past his collar bone, then trimmed it up in the Mexican style where it showed black as the Jack of Clubs. Then out again, graying at the edges. He spent all of his life under the open sky and ate plenty good, so his hair grew fast. Damned if I could guess how he'd present himself each time I saw him—his beard like a river otter stretching out lazy across a rock or curling up fast if danger approached.

Once I finished cursing him out, Doc jammed his big gun home into its holster and got ready to mount up and leave—without the animals we so much coveted. "I'll see you around, August John. But before I go, I need the five-spot back."

In the face of Doc's loaded gun, I decided five dollars wasn't worth dying over. So I gave him back his money.

Doc saluted me as he led his horse out to the prairie, and I called him a dirty name.

"Seems like a man like you oughtn't to make any new

enemies," I said. " 'Specially since a man like me's a benefit to your trade."

Another quick salute.

"I can ear dog a bronc and balance a throw-back better'n anybody you saw. And no jail can hold me, Oregon boot or no." Which was a fart in the wind because I'd never been inside a jail cell in my life nor laid eyes on the heavy iron clamp they sometimes stuck on the road agents up North.

But I had some truth on my side. "I've snookered ponies from Spotted Tail himself and can sneak ' in and out of a hidey-hole slick as sheep dip. I'm the prince of the Niobrara country."

Doc must've liked that one because when he walked back to confront me again, he spoke with exaggerated generosity.

"I didn't realize I was in the presence of such royalty."

"Ho-ho." He had this way of trying to be funny.

But the joke was on him.

With both hands, I grabbed the pitchfork I'd been leaning on and quicker than you can say "jack rabbit," I had it pressed solid against Doc's chest.

His eyes liked to fell out of his head with excitement.

I jabbed him with the fork. "Now it's your turn to toe the dirt, Mr. Jim Cherry, or should I call you Texas Jack Lyons? Where'd you come up with the name 'Middleton' any-hoo?"

Well, his real name was Jim Riley, and not everything about Doc was a lie.

He truly was from Texas. He killed James Keefe in Sidney, and a Wyoming stock detective named Lykins was out to get him.

Hell, when you think on it a while, we were all out to get him, one way or another—as friend or enemy—and nearly all of us succeeded in one way or another.

Even the pissant little Dutch detective had the upper hand sometimes—Lykins, the rotten back-stabbing bastard.

Right there in the livery stable in Julesburg, I made Doc hand me his gun. When I had him all helpless at the business end of my pitchfork, I asked if him and me might join up.

He got a real kick out of me saying it.

"What you told me before is true, isn't it, Gus? You aren't scared of me one little bit, are you?"

Sitting there, looking down the handle of my fork, I thought about the situation I was in. What if Doc pulled out another weapon in surprise, as I had? He certainly might. What would I do?

Would I run him through with the steel tines?

Would I put Jim Cherry underground for good and become known as the man who killed Doc Middleton?

Even at fourteen years old, I recognized how long life might become defending such a title.

And how short.

"Truth is," I said, propping the pitchfork up against the wall, "right now, I'm more scared of myself."

Doc nodded like I said something real profound.

"Hell, Gus," he said. "You and me both."

Afterwards, me and Doc got along pretty well, and before long two or three others came along on the road back down the Niobrara—Flyspeck Billy and Dill Schiller and Albert Wade, too, I guess, for a while. We skimmed some horses off the edge of the Red Cloud agency and by then had quite a herd. Naturally Albert started cutting up every chance he got, showing off and acting the clown. We sold them horses to a rancher named Olive.

Two years later, things were still the same.

It's what I thought at the time: nothing had changed by 1879.

Now I think I was wrong.

Chapter Two

I remember running horses off the Pine Ridge agency again in the summer of '79, and in the middle of the yipping and thunder and dust and hell, Albert swung his legs over the barrel to ride his buckskin cayuse sideways like a girl, showing off.

Riding bareback, he nearly fell. I'll tell you—if he would've gone under, it would've been the end of Kid Wade, mashed up under sixty times four pounding hooves. And where would I be now?

But we all laughed until our guts hurt—me and Windy Barnes and Dill Schiller. Albert was so cute. Poor Windy almost coughed up a lung.

Boots Harper gave up a smirk, so you know it was funny.

Windy, Boots, and Dill rode the flanks of the wild drove while Albert and me meandered all over behind the critters, making catcalls, pushing the bunch of pintos and roans, piebalds and buckskin mares east to the creek south of Holt Ranch where they could cool their cleft paws before trailing the Keya Paha rough country. Albert wore his hairy old shotgun chaps, and I covered my legs with a set of Mexican leather armas, cowhide hanging down from my roan's saddle forks to ward off the Russian bull thistles.

We imagined we were real live cowboys.

"Lookee me—I kin fly." Albert with his heels pulled up to his gelding's withers and arms outstretched. The silly sumbitch.

I had tears in my eyes, laughing so hard, but I sported a bug on, too. "Damn you, hold on."

I kept imagining his corpse, chopped to gristle.

Dill's arm was a pinwheel, cheering Al forward. "Wahooo!"

Boots just shook his head before spurring on up the line. He was a few years older than the rest of us, and it showed in his attitude.

Albert Wade was as good at trick riding as he was at almost everything else. No more'n five and a half feet tall and maybe a hundred and thirty pounds, he didn't like a saddle, wouldn't stick to it if he had one.

His old man was a bronc buster and frowned on men who clutched at their gear to hold on. Al once told me, "I won't ever be accused of pulling leather on a saddle horn."

So he didn't use a saddle.

But he wore those chaps. And a half-breed holster buttoned to his belt.

The gun he carried was a Colt new double-action .38 revolver, and the barrel stuck out from the leather's open end. Al said his gun was called "Lightning," and there was a .41-caliber version called "Thunderer" he wanted to get. "Then I'll bring the storm where'er I go."

He brushed a dollop of thick sandy-brown hair from his defiant blue eyes and cackled like a rooster.

Back then, I guess a lot of men wanted Colts and said so. I sometimes still carried a little gun in my boot. Sometimes I didn't.

Ahead of us, the golden sun dipped from a ceramic blue sky into flares of oranges and pinks. A flirty hot breeze rolled in from the hills, ripe with the smell of sage and horse apples. Far as we could see in all directions, we owned a landscape of burnished copper-green bluestem ankle high in April. Somewhere up ahead, the jagged slash of the Niobrara waited for us.

I guess you could say everything that was to follow got started that evening on the river.

Or maybe everything started to end.

Some of us went to jail afterwards, and some of us moved on. Some of us died, and some lived, and them who lived ain't always done so well ever since then.

We should've seen it all coming, I suppose. Maybe we wouldn't have lost so much.

Some things you never lose.

Run sixty frothy broomsticks through a hot Nebraska day, you'll never lose the smell.

And I ain't never lost Kid Wade's voice in my head.

"Pick up y'r britches, you damned sheepherders."

Raised around horses and cows, Albert didn't know a sheepherder from tobaccy dip.

It was just something he liked to say when he wanted to sound tough.

"Sit up high, you sheepherders! Don't build a shed around it, sheepherders!"

It got sorta sing-songy, him calling everybody a sheepherder.

I didn't mind. Albert kept us on track. It's what I needed then—somebody to keep me honest. Not honest to any sense of morals and certainly not to the law, which didn't exist for us anyway.

Not honest to pals who wandered in and out of our circle, but honest to life in general and youth and to the piss and vinegar charging through our veins.

Albert made sure we didn't lose sight of our goal. Which was, ultimately I suppose, to have no goals at all other than taking in as much of everything as it came to us.

"The sun's down soon, and supper's waiting on me. How 'bout you, August John?"

With the sandhills blowing in so much grit, we like to ate a topsoil supper already, but there's no arguing my guts were rumbling. In those days, I'd eat a rattlesnake and wash it down with a cup of venom.

I dropped back through the horses to rein in beside Al and still had to yell over the whinnying to be heard.

"We get these animals to Holt crick, I'll fry the eggs."

"You make coffee. I'll fry the eggs."

Last time we were together in camp, I made the eggs runny.

By God, Al got so mad, I was scared he was gonna turn his damn holster on me.

I cleared some dust from my throat and spat. "Hell of a day, ain't it?"

The sun winked through a parade of tall clouds, crowning their shoulders with light like epaulets on a cavalry of indigo and blue. Union boys. Even the sky was red-blooded American.

Albert agreed. "Hell of a day, Gus."

The Indian horses swung around in a graceful curve, wild but orderly, sticking together through ancient instincts, slowing their pace as the trail began to gently roll.

"Yip, yip, yip!" Dill and Boots pointed the string off to the south.

I liked it when Albert called me Gus. I didn't know it yet, but I wasn't quite as proud of August John as I'd been the day outside Julesburg with Doc Middleton.

"How much farther to the crick?"

Al sniffed the wind. "Say a half hour this way, then around them hills out yonder." He knew his directions. "A man is truly alive on days like today, Gus."

"Damn right." There was no better air to breathe, no better friend to ride with.

Al was always keeping watch.

"You seen anybody following us?"

"Sure. You?"

"Maybe," Al said.

"Couple Sioux braves back there, maybe a mile behind us."

"Trouble?"

"No, sirree."

"I didn't think so, neither."

"They ain't got the stones for it."

"I reckon not."

"Yah, yah!" Albert pushed off then, driving his buckskin left to cut a fussy yellow dun back into the herd, but not soon enough. The stray mustang shot back west, hell-for-leather, its tail whirling crazy in the wind.

Albert flashed me a grin, whipped around, and whistled, waving me on with the others.

He bulled after the loner on his own.

I turned back to the rumbling stream of horseflesh, signaled Dill to lend Albert a hand.

I didn't want him going it by himself.

In those days, none of us boys thought of Albert as this great horse rustler Kid Wade or "Slippery Jack" like he called himself, because to us he was just our pal, and we knew Deborah, his mother, and we knew his old man.

We were Pony Boys, and because of Al, we took sixty horses from the Indians, and wouldn't Doc be pleased?

It meant some nice hard coin in our pockets, and maybe one of the church girls would finally give me the time of day.

Al was a good fellow to have around, experienced and tough. He'd been in jail once up Sioux Falls way, in Dakota territory, but he escaped sure as one day follows the next. They were lookin' for him in Iowa, too, on account of some old nag he took the previous fall from a man named Leonard.

While Dill loped after Al, I gigged my roan ahead to take up the running flank, opposite Windy Barnes. Windy was fat and clumsy and had the vapors, and sometimes he'd go into coughing fits with the kind of dust we were raising. Which is why I didn't send him back to catch up with Al.

A couple young colts, all legs and no sense, splintered off in front of me, but I circled out and coaxed them back onto the trail, careful so they wouldn't turn a hoof. The ground was getting lumpy the farther we came down off the flats into the river's rough brush country.

"Let 'em slow up," I said. "Take it easy."

Windy heard me and gave off an involuntary bark—lung stuff. He pounded his chest with a gloved fist. He was the weakest one of us. Probably getting sunstroke from not wearing a hat. And the only one wearing gloves.

He shouldn't have been out there.

But we rode on and almost made it to the crick before Albert and Dill came back from chasing their stray.

By golly, they had four between 'em, but not one of them was the cantankerous dun. Instead, they chased along a quartet of the most beautiful notch-eared buckskins I ever saw. These weren't no weak fish. Their muscles rippled, liquid under a film of short-cropped hair and sweat. The lead horse blowed through her nose and tossed her head around. A real beaut, and the boys brought her and her fellows into the herd like fine gardeners arranging a bouquet.

"Did you see the Indians?" I said.

"I seen 'em," said Dill.

Albert hooked a thumb in Dill's direction. "One look at his mug and they ran for next week."

You couldn't help but laugh. Nobody'd call Dill Schiller pretty.

"Where'd you find the four buckskins?"

Albert just grinned.

At Holt Creek, Doc had a lean-to set up between two old cottonwoods next to a roughhewn corral with a makeshift cattle race. There were shadowy bundles of flies over the banks of the spring-fed river, and already the spring peepers were trilling out a chorus at a nearby pool. Spring was gettin' on to summer.

Doc liked the indiscrete creeks, scrawny tributaries of the Niobrara or Keya Paha. Plum Creek, Bone Creek, or Long Pine. Rock Creek was a favorite where he had a house, or Laughing Water, where he was betrayed by Lykins and Llewellyn.

We got the animals penned in and watered at Holt, and our own horses hobbled in the grass before dark. Weren't no use in brushing them down as we intended to keep a'going soon as we had a nice rest.

The cottonwoods' silver leaves rustled against the night. A few stars sparked to life.

I had to relieve myself, and I got away from the bunch. When I came back, I saw Boots was off to one side, jawing with Windy. Had his arm around his shoulder, real friendly like.

What could those two be talking about?

Albert said, "Let's break out some grub," and he directed Dill to drop our war bag under one of the trees.

Thinking about them Indians, I thought we maybe oughtn't to start a fire so we wouldn't be seen. Just in case anybody else showed up.

"Makes me no never mind if we've got a fire or not," Albert said. Nobody argued.

I was relieved not to be frying any eggs.

Sitting around in the dark, we ate pretty good. I tucked away enough lard cracklins and molasses bread to get by anyway.

Before long, the moon was skirting the horizon.

Boots passed around a jug. I think I snoozed a little.

Later on, them old braves came up after us, but we told 'em we hadn't seen any horse thieves.

In the moonlight, they damn well saw the horses in the corral, but they likewise saw Albert's gun.

Them two being all alone like that, they slunk away like whipped skunks. Dill yelled after 'em to send us some squaws, and for a while I wondered if they would, and what Dill would do then if the girls showed up.

But there weren't any girls, just the five of us under the trees with Little Wound's horses in a thistle patch below the trail.

Boots and Windy sitting tight together like old chums. Which still struck me as odd, but I was soon to find out something.

Around midnight, Boots said, "Let's take this bunch down to Hampton's cabin," meaning a place on the Niobrara about a mile above Morris's Crossing, what they later called Carns.

Windy said the cabin sounded good to him, but Dill voted for Richardson's ranch because Henry's daughter was sweet on Doc, and Dill was always trying to get in good with Doc.

Albert said he had a better idea. He said he had a new hideout in one of the brushy cedar canyons straight on east along the Keya Paha—a place Doc didn't know about. I guess Al knew about a standing corral there.

Maybe something his dad built and left behind.

Al's dad was always leaving stuff behind.

Including Al.

When Al said Doc didn't know about his hidey hole, I felt the cracklins sour just a bit in my guts.

In those days, Doc Middleton was top dog just about everywhere in the unorganized territory west. Hell, there wasn't any government other than a justice of the peace, and he was a coon's age away.

Pine Ridge was easy pickings for him; Rosebud was a breeze. A boon for Doc, trading stolen native horses for freight with teamsters on the Black Hills trail at Morris's Crossing. Sometimes he'd trade way over at Paddock on Eagle Creek, sometimes venturing off as far as O'Neill City on the Elkhorn.

Top dog, all right, but Al said we deserved some scraps for ourselves.

The idea of holding out on Doc wasn't new to me.

"We'll shack up at my hideout for a day or two," Al said, "sort through the herd, then move on to Doc's place."

I stuck up for Albert, and maybe I shouldn't have, because it was the kind of thing put me in dutch with the others. "I like Al's idea. Where's this corral at?"

"It's a place called Pleasant Valley Station just west of where the Keya Paha flows into the Running Water." Which was what the Indians called the Niobrara.

Dill gave Al a grumpy face.

He was sucking off Middleton's tit and kept pressing for Henry Richardson's place.

"I never heard of no Pleasant Valley," he said.

"Don't forget Boots suggested Hampton's," Windy said. Coughing.

I scolded everybody but Al. "You fellows ought to be thinking ahead. Stay one step in front of everybody, including Black Jack Nolan, including Doc Middleton's gang." Like I was older than my sixteen years.

Like it was me who was somebody's dad.

Dill said, "Ain't we Doc Middleton's gang? Ain't we the Pony Boys?"

"Some are."

"Who cares what anybody calls us? I do whatever I want," Albert said.

"Next thing you'll be marching us all the way to Knox County," Dill said.

I told him it wasn't the worst idea.

"Lotta damned Czechs over there, coming in from Iowa, looking to stake a claim. They're gonna need teams to pull wagons and plows."

Albert liked selling to Czech farmers almost as much as Black Hills traders.

They kept their mouths shut. Plus they had money.

"One time this old sodbuster offered me and Albert a hundred dollars in gold coins for a couple broke-down nags," I said. "He didn't know what American money was worth."

I didn't tell them Doc would never have let the kraut overpay like he did for the swaybacks, but Al never had a problem with his conscience. I guess back then I didn't either.

The sodbuster wanted the horses real bad, so he got 'em.

Cleaning up the last of his lard cracklins, Albert said, "I guess we'll take this bunch over to Pleasant Valley after all."

"I think you're wrong to do it," Boots said.

"You can think all you want."

"I'm with Al," I said.

Boots's face under the moon wasn't so much mad as disappointed.

He looked at me like my mom when I left our place the year before. The day I told her to go to hell and meant every word.

"I'm gonna have to disagree with you, Albert. You too, August John."

My stomach rolled over the way he said it. Boots using my nickname left me shook up.

Nobody said a word.

After a while, Albert said, "Let's mount up."

"I ain't going," Boots said.

Albert screwed up his face. "You ain't riding out alone."

Boots agreed. "I ain't. Windy's with me."

"You two ain't leaving. Not tonight, you ain't. Later on, next week, you might do such a thing. We need every one of us to keep these here horses running straight."

Boots didn't bother arguing. He just gave a sort of chuckle and stood up, strolled over to his horse, and set her forelocks free. Then he climbed into his seat. He had a simple wooden Mexican saddle. I imagined his butt was pretty sore after riding all day.

Here he was fixing to ride off into the night.

"Reckon we'll take our share of the horses." Then he talked to Windy. "You coming with me or not?"

He rode over toward the half-assed pen and undid the gate. Around twenty critters streamed out onto the silvery open range—including the four buckskins with notches in their ears.

Windy started coughing.

I slapped his back. "Hush up."

But Windy couldn't hush up, and in less than a minute he was hacking and gagging, and Dill had him by one shoulder while I steered him along by the other. Like trying to guide a blind cow. We got him down into the crick water and dippered tin cans up for him to sip.

Windy sagged under my grip but croaked, "Good God, enough water, boys. You'd like to drown me," and the cough lightened up some.

Then he plodded over to his horse and climbed on top. He got around Boots's horses and started driving them away.

Boots touched the rim of his hat. "You all take care, Pony Boys."

Boots never carried a gun. One of his many mistakes.

Albert jumped up and took two steps toward him. Put his hand to his holster, swinging it up around the single button on his belt. The end of the leather was open so the barrel of his Colt stuck out, aimed flat at Boots.

"I ain't gonna let you take them horses, Boots. 'Specially not the buckskins."

"Like hell." Boots turned his back and rode around the drove, and when he did, he waved at Windy to take up the slack.

If Boots ever looked back at us, I'll never know.

I had my eyes nailed to Albert.

He stood alone in the dark, staring out across the high plains, his slender hand on the half-breed holster, the muzzle of his gun aimed at the shrinking specks of black near the horizon. His hand trembled, and the muzzle shook. But Al didn't shoot.

Boots had some kind of nerve. And Windy with him.

We mounted up in complete silence.

I wished Boots would've left us his jug.

It was after that night, more often than not, Albert and me started leaving the other fellows out of our plans, even Dill.

Before long, I got to thinking it was the two of us alone who were Pony Boys, and everybody else, including Doc Middleton and the rest, could go hang.

And you know what? Well, some of them sumbucks did hang. Sooner than we ever imagined.

Chapter Three

The sun was plenty high before our horses drowned their fetlocks in the Keya Paha at a low spot and shoved us along into Pleasant Valley, the dragonflies swooping loops around our heads. It wasn't so much a valley as a scrub-filled ravine with a hardwood forest sprouting up from the floor like hair from a whore's armpit. A dog came bounding out across the range to meet us in the hot forenoon, and his voice was welcoming.

"Howdy, McGee," Albert said to the dog. "Men, this here is Moses McGee."

He was a patchwork quilt of a beast, knee high with coarse brown hair patches stitched over black and white for a crazy-looking whole. He weighed maybe fifty pounds soaking wet. Nimble and poison quick.

I doffed my hat to the cur. Dill snickered and tried to tag him with a stream of tobacco spit.

"McGee's too quick for you, Dill," Albert said. "A born guard dog."

With McGee yapping and nipping at their hooves, we funneled the Indian horses down a deep ravine between two long, tall hills of sod, then through a shelter belt of cedar trees thick as Noah's beard, like to tear my skin off riding through. Albert just catcalled and teased me and Dill along into the station.

"My heavens, you sheepherders got to grow tougher hides," Al said.

Much as I loved Mother Nature, she could be a prickly, painful bitch with a stockyard full of malicious barbs.

Like all mothers. She really didn't give a shit about us.

Once out of the scraggly woods, we let the horses spread out onto four or five acres of bunch grass and weeds. I tried to get a count, but they were moving around, still restless. "Looks like thirty-nine."

Dill muttered, "I get thirty-eight."

"Forty on the button," Albert said. "The cedars and brush makes for a natural fence. By and by we'll get sorted into Trudy's pens."

Trudy?

Dill stuck out his lower lip and folded his arms in the saddle. "Who's this now? Hang fire a second. Who's this Trudy?"

"Trudy's my cousin. She manages the station."

"Bullroar."

"Bull-nothing. She is so my cousin. You tell him, Gus."

I offered Dill a good-natured shrug. "If she's got a pan of beans, she's good enough for me."

I had no idea if Al was talking true or not. He likely had kin all over the place, including a couple sisters. But I had never heard of anybody named Trudy.

Having stayed awake all night, I was too tired to care.

Dill decided to push it.

"Listen, Albert—you already let half the profits go with Boots and Windy. Be damned if you give away another share. Doc ain't gonna like none of it."

Albert didn't like Dill's tone of voice. "In case maybe you ain't noticed, Doc isn't here."

He put his fingers close to his holster again. If he seemed to be more interested in his gun than ever before, I didn't notice right then. Later on, I did.

Dill shut up though, not because of the holster, but because Kid Wade was right.

Doc, Boots, and Windy. All the rest who sometimes came along—Black Hank and Richard Bryant, who they called Limber Dick. Count Shevaloff and Black George, Curley Grimes and Jack Nolan.

They weren't none of them there.

Not a one.

We were separated by vast swathes of land and sky and hours of travel, and our word was gospel.

Sitting like a fly speck in the middle of the pasture, it felt like nobody was anywhere.

As I watched the horse herd spread a dark stain into the lonely sea of yellow grass, it was like we were all alone in the whole entire world.

I tried to imagine Doc Middleton with his haughty swagger and scruffy whiskers, his big old gold tooth shining like a beacon out there someplace . . . but I couldn't.

Him being out there, us being here—none of it seemed real.

Me being more tired than I thought.

It was—in some ways—like even I wasn't there. Like I was some stranger watching myself from a distance, way up high.

Albert clucked his horse into taking a few steps away from us. He glanced over his shoulder. "You boys wait here. I'll rustle up Trudy and see if she's got those beans."

For the first time, I noticed the dark line of a stream coming off from the south, just a little trickling branch of rain squeezins, nothing that would even have a proper name. I imagined stream water flowing into the bigger cricks and the Keya Paha, then to the Niobrara and on past Old Baldy close to where they now built the town of Lynch until it curved up north to hook into the Missouri.

Old Baldy's a big chalk rock hill jutting out of the ground on the Missouri bluffs. Them early river hounds Lewis and Clark discovered it almost a hundred years ago, and when they found a prairie dog city there, they made a big old holler because nobody but the Indians ever seen prairie dogs before them.

Well, plenty of Christian people had seen prairie dogs ever since.

When I think of home, I never think of she who bore me, but always Old Baldy.

Looking around, I decided Pleasant Valley would make a nice home.

In front of the small stream stood a house with a privy, a barn, and the corral.

Albert bounced on his horse across the landscape toward the set of toy buildings, and I speculated on the layout with Dill.

"Those must be the pens he wants to sort the horses into."

"The pens you and me are going to sort horses into. Kid Wade ain't gonna do nothing but loaf, same as always."

Dill was just being rotten since we weren't going to Richardson's place.

I whistled "Blue Belle Dumplings" while we waited but couldn't get the tune right, so I took a snooze. At least I think I must've slept because it wasn't three seconds and Albert was back crowing at me.

"You want beans, Trudy's got beans."

"Good old Trudy," Dill said, dry and mean. Seemed like he was gonna carry on all day.

We followed the trail, and Kid Wade led us into the station yard.

I parked my roan in front of the old barn, more awake now, feeling a little bit fresh after my nap.

The barn was likely twenty feet tall or thereabouts with a hayloft inside, crooked with all the logs sticking out on the corners, sharp like Indian spears. Damn thing was so out of plumb, it made you dizzy if you looked at it long enough.

Later on, when I leaned against the wall, it seemed solid enough.

Across the way, the house wasn't any nicer to look at.

If God dropped a pile of sticks from heaven and filled the in-between with mud, you'd have Pleasant Valley station.

But give it this—it had a tin roof, and a bright-red water pump outside with a cold steel pipe drilled directly into the ground. I asked Albert who paid for such extravagance. "Nobody," he said, which meant *don't ask any questions.*

"You all can put your horses inside the barn, across from the little polled heifer," Albert said. "You'll find grain there and a trough for water." A passel of chickens swarmed around, and a mean looking rooster chased Moses McGee into a yipping retreat toward the house.

"Damned rooster's always on fire over somebody."

"How often you get over this way?" I asked Al, because he'd never mentioned it to me.

"Time or two," is all he said.

I dismounted, and McGee came back around, circling me with a happy, wagging dance. I reached down to scratch his ears, and he went limp to the ground, taking in the mush with a contented sigh.

Some guard dog.

Albert said, "We came at the right time, boys. Trudy's got a whole damn storehouse inside there. It's a regular mercantile express."

"Who's the wagon?" Dill said, poking his chin toward the space between the house and barn where a high-wheeled buckboard waited with a couple mares strapped to a hitch. It was parked far enough back you couldn't see it on the trail's approach.

"Like I say," Al said, "Trudy does a business."

He used an odd tone of voice.

Dill let fly with a stream of tobaccy.

I turned around to scratch an itch and hitch up my trousers, and Dill shuffled over. He wore a scowl the way some men wore a mustache.

"You don't know this Trudy from Queen Esther, do you?"

"I don't. But I guess it doesn't matter none."

"Matter's to me. I don't like any of this. Albert's acting like them horses are all his. You and me got some say in this. I went along to the rez 'cause I thought we was workin' for Doc."

He'd worked himself into a lather. Now he was snorting around like he was fixin' to sprout peaked ears and a hairy mane all his own.

Dill could be a pill when he wanted to be, and it looked like he wanted to be one now, so I tried to calm him down some. "Don't be in a stew. I reckon Doc will see some profit from these horses, eventually. It ain't like Al to shut out Doc all the way."

But Dill wasn't having it.

"I don't think the Kid has any intention of sharing this run with Doc at all. Not after Boots and Windy already took the cream off the top. I especially don't like Albert bringing in another person. And a woman on top of it. You said yourself you didn't know no *Trudy.*"

"I don't figure he's bringing Trudy into anything."

"Oh, no? What do you call it?"

"If she's his cousin—"

"She ain't."

Dill was awfully sure of himself. We both turned our attention back to Albert. He was standing beside the buckboard now, kicking at the dirt only a few steps away from the mares, and I could hear voices coming from the front of the house. A man's voice, thick and slow with words, and a higher pitched tone.

"I sure do thank you, ma'am."

"Oh, sure. Of course. Think nothing of it."

"You're a peach is what you are."

"And you're a plum."

They came around the corner of the house arm in arm, an old man and a girl. When the man saw Albert, all the fruity talk stopped, and he retrieved his arm from Trudy. He was dressed in a cotton shirt with no buttons and the arms cut off. Underneath, he wore a long-sleeved wrapping of eggshell-white long underwear with gray stains of sweat. His wool trousers were brown and fit loose around his apple-basket gut. His shoes were losing their soles, and he wore a round, small-brimmed hat over huge cotton clumps of hair.

Trudy took a step to his left, and if I didn't know her, I sure as hell knew him. Sonny Clausen was an old rum drummer from Paddock. A man who never knew a stranger.

The cracks around his puffy red eyes crinkled with his cheeks, a topographical map of a happy drunk's life story.

He shoved his hand forward. "By-de-Gawd, if it ain't Albert Wade."

Al ignored the greeting.

Clausen's eyes went from Albert's face to the gun buttoned to his belt. Then back to his face. "Didn't reckon on seeing you today." Sonny craned his neck to look over me and Dill. "August John and Dill Schiller with you."

"Howdy, Clausen." I gave him a quick nod and nothing else. Nothing to get ahold of. Nothing to build a castle around. If you said "boo" to the old devil, he'd pick it up and run with it. You'd be standing there next week listening to him talk.

Sonny kept trying to stoke up a chat, showing us his wooden teeth with an enthusiastic grin. "How you boys been doing?" He tipped his hat backwards on a high white hairline. "How's your pa, Albert?"

"Ain't seen him in forever."

"The hell. Well, it's a real shame. Always liked your pa."

"Makes one of us."

More showing of the teeth, and this time, Clausen gave up a laugh. "You tell him I owe him a tall beer one day on account of the pump he dropped off last week."

Nobody said anything, and a big horsefly buzzed around between us. The old man wiped at his forehead with the back of his sleeve. You could smell him ten feet away, like sour peat moss. Trudy swatted at the fly.

The buckboard carried an oblong pine box, the size of a coffin. Its rough lid was full of knots and carried an overabundance of nails.

"Gonna be a scorcher today, eh?" Clausen said, fitting his cap more tightly around his skull.

Then: "Been meaning to look about your ma, Gus."

I ignored the pleasantry.

"Me and your dad were at Fort Randall together." His lips made a firm, tight line. "Guess it was a long time ago. You never really knew your dad, did you, Gus? How old were you when he passed?"

When we continued to refuse him the conversation he craved, Clausen crawled up onto his bench seat. "Okay, boys. Well, I guess I'll let you go."

Trudy took one step toward the wagon. "Stay well, Mr. Clausen."

Clausen acted like he didn't hear her. Instead, he started pitching his nonsense again. The old devil couldn't help it.

"I was just telling Trudy what a scorcher it was going to be. Hard on the livestock, for sure." He closed one eye and leaned down to peer at me from under his cap. "You look in on Trudy's heifer for her? She's gonna calf anytime. Your old dad was magic with cows."

"Why don't you look in on her?"

"I said I would, but I'm already late for my old lady's supper."

"You mean breakfast?"

Clausen glanced over his shoulder at Trudy. Then he sent me a wink.

"I guess I mean supper. From last night."

Trudy told him to go to hell, and they both laughed.

Al wasn't laughing. "Trudy's my cousin," he said, matter of fact.

Dill poked my ribs with his elbow. "She's everybody's cousin."

I had continued to eye the oblong box, and my curiosity finally got the best of me. "What'cha buying today, Clausen?"

"Nothing concerns you, August John. I guess my needs have been met."

I wasn't sure if he was talking about the box behind him or not.

Al spun on his bootheel, turned his attention to Trudy. He always told us he was sixteen, but I figured him for a couple years older. Trudy was maybe ten more.

"What's all this talk about a cow?"

She waved him off with a flutter. "Don't you fret about it," she said. "Sonny always worries about a heifer's first calf."

"I don't want you going without a good cow. And the calf will bring you more later on."

Trudy put her hand on Al's shoulder. "You're sweet to worry."

At my elbow, Dill cursed under his breath. I gave him a sidelong look as if to say, *What's up?*

He nodded, and I followed his eyes. Saw the problem.

Clausen had stopped talking.

And he wasn't listening to Trudy and Al.

Instead, from his vantage point on the buckboard, he sat looking over the field at Little Wound's horses. The more his eyeballs darted around over the herd, the faster his jaw started to work. Like he was chewing a cud.

"You boys bring them critters in today?" he said.

"I don't know what you mean," I told him.

"What's there, about thirty of 'em?"

"We got no idea what you're talking about, Sonny."

Clausen stood up tall on the wagon floor and put the flat of his hand to the brim of his hat.

"Heard about a man west of here who's missing four buckskins. Those horses out there," he said,. "those look to be Indian ponies?"

"You must be seeing things."

"I don't think so . . ."

Dill's voice hung low as the devil's toenails and sounded just as sharp. "There ain't no horses out there, Clausen."

The old man's face flushed white. He got Dill's message.

This time when he spoke, his voice was pinched and high. "I don't mean to be poking into your business."

He had overstepped, and he knew it.

"Maybe I wasn't clear," said Dill.

Clausen nodded. "Oh, why . . . y-yes you were, Dill. Yes, you were." He swallowed hard, and his Adam's apple went up and down like a woodpecker's red-feathered scalp.

I asked Clausen if he knew his bugle calls. "They must've taught you some bugle calls out at Fort Randall?"

"I reckon so."

I put as much menace into my voice as I could. "There's a time a man ought to stand his ground. There's a time to retreat."

"I hear you."

"We got no business in horses," Dill said. "You must be thinking about somebody else."

"My mistake, boys."

"Ain't I right, Albert? We don't have any business in horses, do we?"

Albert wagged his chin like all of us were crazy. "Enough rough talk. You boys need to get inside and eat some beans," he said.

Looking up at Clausen, he offered him a generous salute. "You travel safe with your long box, Mr. Clausen."

"I'll be careful."

"Men been known to have accidents traveling the Elkhorn road. Real dangerous."

But Al had pushed Clausen as far as he could. The old man was no weak sister.

"You best be careful yourself, Albert."

"Always am."

Al swung his arm around Trudy's shoulders and pulled her tight against him as he held Clausen's gaze. She stood a foot taller than him.

The four of us watched the freight wagon trundle back along the trail, out of the valley.

Now our tails were cooked, and we all knew it, even if Al wasn't letting on.

Clausen's flapping yapper was sure to spread the word about Kid Wade and August John driving a bunch of critters around the Keya Paha. If Doc didn't immediately hear about the Pleasant Valley stockyard, a dozen homesteaders in the area would for sure.

Dill didn't stop cursing under his breath until Clausen was out of sight.

As for Albert and Trudy . . . well, they hadn't seen each other in a real long time.

I stood around at loose ends while their lips got reacquainted.

It could be she wasn't his cousin after all.

Later on, Dill and me got the horses put up at a hardwood stable beside the rugged-looking barn, seven ponies to a stall.

Inside the house, we ate some beans and sipped some coffee. The bad news came around mid-afternoon.

Chapter Four

The homesteader Otto Randolph and his wife, Nora, were looking for a good workhorse. They had a hardpan homestead north of Morris's Crossing someplace and were looking toward putting in a spring row crop.

The Randolphs traveled light, in a snappy wagon with a snow-white bonnet, and I'm here to tell you, I ain't never seen no two pioneers so clean. Nary a piece of grit under their well-trimmed nails, nor stain on their pants. Nora Randolph wore britches just like Otto, but with a big hooded sun bonnet so's you could tell the difference between them.

They didn't have any kids, and they refused to come inside, "Preferring to stand," Nora said, "after the long, bumpy ride from Niobrara City, where my people stay."

Everything about them was sewed up and neat-as-you-please.

Even the gentleman's straw hat sported a thick shellacking of glistening oil.

Trudy's neighbor had told the Randolphs to stop at Pleasant Valley station to pick up a few supplies, so it's what they did. When they got to talking with Albert about horses, he said he might be able to help 'em out.

The piebald he led over was surprisingly tame and didn't balk at his leather braided hackamore.

"This here's about the best horse you're gonna find anywhere."

Otto pinched his chin and looked down his nose. "I seen better."

"You'd be a liar for saying so," Al said.

"Mebbe."

"Nora needs to fill the larder. I've got a list." Otto handed his wife a piece of paper and told her to go inside with Trudy. "Go ahead and add three cans of peaches, if you please."

I gave it two seconds thought and decided to follow the women inside.

Al didn't need my help pushing off the piebald, and since I hadn't been around civilization awfully much lately, I was curious what news Nora Randolph might have.

Trudy's station house was the length of two wagon teams and maybe twenty feet wide with a hard swept dirt floor and wax-paper windows to let in a sorta tan-colored murky sunlight. The place was divided evenly in half by a wall, the front room being a public station.

Inside the back room was Trudy's bed and chest of drawers, but I didn't see back there until a couple nights later.

In the front room, perpendicular to the front door, down the full length of one log-built wall, ran a series of tightly packed shelves with a hardwood counter in front. The shelves were mostly empty, but three or four were full enough with tins of beans, tomatoes, and fruit as to make them sag. Trudy carried sacks of flour and jars of sorghum, and I guess if a lady wanted to outfit a kitchen there were some utensils and pans and such for sale hanging from the center post.

Inside, Dill Schiller was sipping coffee from a tin cup at a round dining table built from pine scraps with a downhill slope to the west. The supper chairs were nothing but three-legged stools.

Trudy scurried back and forth behind the counter, mouthing "Yes, ma'am," and "Not today, ma'am," and "Please let me check, ma'am," and all sorts of platitudes that had me laughing.

Dill gave me the skunk eye, like *what's so funny?*

"She sounds like she's playing store," I said.

"Well, hell, where do you think we are?" He acted all defensive, and I wondered if he was taking a shine to Trudy.

When I turned my attention back to the women, Nora was busy jawboning to nobody in particular, addressing all of us in the room.

"The way Otto's got it figured, folks can't start stocking up too soon for winter. We've got good horses and a cow. Wouldn't mind a few of those chickens I saw outside. I expect we'll pay you a visit here again before harvest."

Trudy liked the sound of it, and when she stopped churning around for a minute and stood in the milky sunshine with a big, wide smile, she was pretty as anything.

Matter of fact, she lifted her hand up to hook a strand of reddish locks behind her ear, and my heart went out to her.

Trudy wore her hair long, draping over her strong shoulders and small, firm breasts like curtains hiding the offering plates at church.

She had a face lightly dusted with freckles, and her teeth were even and accounted for under slim lips and a slender nose.

Every square inch of her was a treasure, and her nutmeg-brown eyes and delicate eyebrows spoke of a tender but confident strength.

I wondered I hadn't seen it earlier.

Maybe Dill already had?

Albert came inside then, followed by Otto. "You'll appreciate the purchase, Mr. Randolph."

I noticed the bulge in the breast pocket of Al's shirt. It's where he always stashed money when somebody paid him. I wondered how much Otto Randolph had paid for the piebald.

The Randolphs settled up with Trudy, then Nora said, "We've

got a pan of blueberry muffins out in the wagon for you."

The Randolphs were the kind of settlers I liked. Tough and sassy.

Czechs who were green with the color of money.

But the gossip they carried was dark blood red.

"S'pose you all don't get a lot of visitors?" Otto said.

Trudy's smile was impish, and for some reason, I didn't care for the expression she used.

"In and out."

"Guess you probably ain't heard, then."

"Heard what?" Dill said.

"Doc Middleton's party was jumped by a yellow-spined Texan out Sidney-way. Man named Charley Reed lured 'em from camp into town. Looks like one of the boys is dead. Maybe two of 'em. Word is it's Doc himself gone to meet the Lord."

Trudy stopped like a marble statue, keeping one hand on the counter and one up by her ear where her fingers locked into place beside her cheek.

Sitting beside me at the room's lone round table, all the air seemed to flow out of Dill, and he quit breathing.

It was like somebody stopped a clock and nobody knew how to start it again.

Finally, Albert said, "It's a lie. You got it wrong, Mister."

Otto put his hand behind his head and tilted back his slick straw hat. "I don't think so. Heard it straight from a fella named Richardson. Maybe you heard of him? Henry Richardson? I understand Doc is sweet on his daughter."

Albert chided him, his voice carrying more than a touch of scorn. "Now I know for sure it's a stretcher. Henry Richardson's upside-down crazy."

"It sounded pretty square to me," Otto said. "Doc left his Red Buck horse with Jim Warner before leaving for Sidney. I talked to Warner. He says if ol' Doc don't come back to Morris's Crossing sometime this week, he's gonna sell Red Buck."

"Naw, I don't believe it," Albert said.

"Me, neither," said Dill, springing back to life like Lazarus in the tomb. "Doc's too crafty to be caught like you're saying. He would never let himself be tricked into going into town at night."

I kept my mouth shut.

Warner was Middleton's friend, and Richardson was nearly his dad-in-law. If they said something about Doc, it sure enough might be true. The Randolphs didn't seem like people who'd cause trouble just for the hell of it.

But with Otto's money in his pocket, Al didn't see any need to be polite.

"Go on now, Mr. Randolph. Get your stuff and move on out of here."

Dill agreed. "Yeah, we don't need folks dropping in with garbage talk."

Otto stroked his chin like I'd seen him do before and looked down his nose at Dill. "Reckon it's hard news to take. Everybody around here likes ol' Doc, don't they?" He turned his attention back to Trudy. "I sure didn't mean to rile anybody up."

"It's all right, Mr. Randolph," Trudy said.

"It ain't either all right," Dill said. "People come in here and besmirch a good man's name."

"Surely sayin' a man's dead isn't besmirching him," Nora said.

Trudy had the Randolphs' items arranged in Nora's basket on the counter and gently pushed it toward them.

Otto picked up the basket, then turned to me and the others. "Like I say, we'll be back."

"You keep your ass away from here, you know what's good for you," said Dill under his breath.

Al just sat watching his shoes, elbows on his knees, hands

folded in front of his nose.

He might've been saying a prayer for Doc, except I knew he wasn't. I knew him well enough to know he'd not go to prayin'.

"You all have a good day," said Otto Randolph before stepping outside. "I'll send Nora in with the muffins. I apologize if I said something wrong."

"Keep your damn muffins," I said, just to let Al know whose side I was on.

Before Dill could follow up, Otto walked outside, closing the door behind him.

With the click of the latch, Trudy came around to the table.

"Do you think what he said might be true? Could it be Doc's been killed?"

"Ain't no way in the world," Dill said. "Goddamn sodbusters running around spreading lies."

Al raised his head, keeping his eyes firm on Dill.

"What if it ain't a lie, Dill? What if he's telling true?"

"Now don't you start too, you loco bastard."

"I mean it."

Dill was up on his heels, shoving Trudy's walnut chair backwards and yelling at Al. "You say it again, and you'll fight me."

"I don't wanna fight you, Dill."

"Then you take back what you said." He turned to look at me. "Tell him, Gus. Tell him to take it back."

I felt sick all over.

"Let's all get out there right now," Dill said. "Let's ride down to Morris's Crossing. I'll bet you anything we find Doc there now. Who's with me?"

"We ain't leaving these horses," said Albert.

"Look at me in the eye, either one of you, and tell me Doc's been killed."

I couldn't do what he asked, couldn't look straight at him.

But I managed to talk. "I guess I figure it just might be true."

Dill lashed out like lightning, sweeping our plates from the table, smashing Trudy's dishes into thick, sloppy shards on the floor. He kicked at my chair, making me jump up. Then he turned around and kicked Trudy's counter. "No," he said, more than once. "No, no, no. He ain't been killed. Ain't none of this right."

Trudy tried to reach out to him, but before she could say anything, he knocked some of the broken plates aside and tromped out the door.

The three of us sat there a long time, me and Albert and Trudy.

After maybe ten minutes, I said I'd go after Dill.

"He'll work it off," Albert said. "He'll be back."

"Or not," I said.

"Or not."

"What if Doc's killed?" Trudy said.

Neither Albert nor me had anything to say, and before awful long, Trudy got up and went for a broom parked in the far corner of the room. I stood up and met her halfway back to the table. "I'll take care of it."

"Thank you, Gus."

"I'll do it," said Al.

"It's okay—"

"I said, I'll do, Gus."

He was smaller than me, and I wasn't ever what you'd call a'scared of him, but when Albert got iron in his voice, I knew it was best to stand back. Him and Dill both had fiery tempers.

I handed over the broom to Kid Wade.

"If there's anything else you need me to do . . . ?" I asked Trudy.

"You might check on the heifer," she said.

"Yes, ma'am, I could maybe check on the heifer."

Albert started a heavy, rough sweeping of the plates Dill broke, and, having received my instructions, I decided it best to retreat to the barn.

Al said it was where we'd be sleeping, so I unpacked my bedroll once I got there.

I wasn't surprised to find Dill's horse gone.

No doubt he was halfway to Morris's Crossing by now.

"Or off to Henry Richardson's place," I told myself. He ought to make either destination before dark.

I couldn't say I was sorry to have him gone.

Now it was just me and Al.

But Trudy, too, I reminded myself and felt a shroud of lonesome drop over me.

After supper, Trudy said she wanted to read her Bible, and Al said we ought to look about the livestock once before bedtime, so I said my goodnights, but he stayed inside a while.

Later on in the barn, after I tended the Indian horses, I showed Al the place I'd prepared for us in the afternoon. The pine and cedar building was longer than it was wide with a central alley and a couple stalls on either side for a total of four pens.

The front bay door stood wide open to the south wind, but the back door was stuck shut in the dirt and grass.

"I put us back there in a corner stall so's we can keep our back to the wall and see all the comings and goings."

Our two horses were in the stall next to us, while the dun cow was in the pen across the alley from them on the other side. She seemed like a gentle thing, bloated with calf, but she had a touch of pink eye with a yellow-green dollop swimming in a raw, pink socket.

If it pained her overmuch, she didn't let on.

Al carried a pail of water in from the pump and, after pouring some to our horses, dumped the remainder over his bare head, scrubbing his face. "Brrrr, cold!"

"Deep well out there," I observed. "Nice pump."

"Yeah. My old man installed the pump for her—which shocked the corn shucks out of me."

"How come it shocked you?"

"Three days' work, and he didn't charge her a penny. My old man wouldn't turn a horse from stomping a cripple."

"Yeah, but . . . I mean her being your cousin and all . . ."

"Oh . . . yeah. Her being my cousin."

We both got a laugh out of it, but he didn't deny it, just kept talking.

Albert was glad to find his bedroll unpacked, and I had carried some bread and sorghum from Trudy's kitchen, so we ate some of it while we talked.

He laid back with his fingers laced behind his head. "I can't do anything else but run horses, Gus. I can't be anybody else than I am."

"Nobody wants you to be."

"It's about the only thing I'm good at. Other than breaking jail. You know, no jail can hold me, Gus."

He'd been in jail twice and slipped out both times.

"It's why I'm called Slippery Jack." But as far as I knew, he was the only one called himself by the name.

Al's canvas war bag laid beside him on the dirt, and he fished around in it for his flask. It was about a third full of liquor. After he took a long pull, he said, "O'course, even us *purfessionals* make mistakes. I sure do regret losing those buckskins to Boots and Windy."

"Those four weren't Sioux horses. They had ear notches," I said. "You never told me where you found them."

"I guess they just wandered into my path."

Then he changed the subject. "I'm thinking about raising a

mustache." He fingered the space under his nose and sat up. "What do you think?"

"I think it wouldn't take long to grow. Your grizzled old charcoal face looks like you need a shave ten minutes after you're finished."

He sank back down. "Yes, sir. A mustache is just the thing for me."

But he never did raise one.

"Did I ever tell you about building a fence for this old devil name of Bozik?"

It was common knowledge Al worked around the elderly Czech's place, doing odd jobs. It was also common knowledge Bozik was a horse thief.

I knew the story, and I knew the ranch in question, back east, south of Niobrara City. But I buttoned my lip and let him tell the tale. He enjoyed it so much.

"Bozik had a horse barn hidden inside a hay pile."

"Must've been a pretty small barn."

"Big damn pile."

He handed me the flask, and I was careful not to kill it.

"Doc's got an entire corral underground at Springview Ranch," I said.

"I was talking about Bozik," Al said. "Nobody could shake him. Not women, not kids. Not the law. I'll tell you—one day this local vigilante band came around. Put a rope around his head and threatened right there to hang him up. But he didn't make a peep about the hay pile. So they left us alone afterwards."

I remember when it happened.

"Me and my mom were neighbors on the other side of Konicek's land."

Albert picked up a shit-eatin' grin and practically yelled.

"Konicek! Damn his eyes. You talk about why I ain't nothing more than what I am. It was old Bozik wanting to fence off his ground from Konicek made me see things straight."

"How so?"

"You know how it is around Old Baldy and back to Niobrara City. Damn oak and cottonwood's hard to work with. So when Bozik gets this fence idea, we haul ass down the Verdigre crick and into this old cedar forest."

I'd heard the story before, but Albert enjoyed telling it. And tonight it seemed to have an added message.

"I helped Bozik fell those trees and skid 'em downstream to the ranch, where we laced 'em into a crossways fence five poles high. Konicek to the west, Bozik to the east." Al fell back onto the sod floor and cupped the back of his head in his hands. "Ain't never worked so hard. My arms and legs liked to have given out three times."

I'd seen the fence once right after it went up, and I said so. It was a right nice fence.

"Then you know what happened to it two weeks later."

"Prairie fire."

"Prairie fire—damned straight. Surged across Konicek's hill straight into the cedar wood, stinking sweet and blazing blue. Nothing left of it but ashes."

Al sat up to emphasize the point.

"All our hard, damned work. Nothing left. Nothing but ashes."

I shook my head, thinking he was done, but this time there was a moral to the story. "I ain't never gonna work so hard again. I swore it to myself."

He lay back down, satisfied with his conclusion. "No, sir. Never again."

Al's breath grew deep then, and heavy, and as I listened to him lightly snore, I wondered about the herd of Indian horses and how we'd need to hay them and haul water in the morning from the creek. I wondered about how hard the work would be. And I wondered who he figured on doing the most of it.

Chapter Five

Not a blessed soul had strayed past the station since Otto Randolph and his wife pulled out, and, with Dill Schiller galloping away to Morris's Crossing, Pleasant Valley was home to the three of us—along with the pink-eye pregnant heifer and Little Wound's roughshod remuda.

We stayed for two days before Kid Wade got tired of watching me lug pails of water to the horses.

Turns out his feet got to itchin'.

Sunrise on the third day, Albert pushed back from the breakfast table with an announcement. "A man can only haul so many buckets of water, pitch so many forkfuls of hay, and eat canned peaches for every meal before he's ready to climb over the next hill."

The next hill was to the east, along the Niobrara, toward Heavy Frahm's cathouse. "A man needs excitement in life, Gus."

I was inclined to agree, not so much about the cathouse, and I wondered aloud about the horses.

"Who's gonna take care of them?"

"Trudy won't mind. For a day or two."

"You told Dill you didn't want to leave them here unattended."

"I tell Dill a lot of silly shit."

Trudy stood up and cleared the table without saying a word.

Watching her carry dishes around, I had to agree with Al.

"Yes, sir . . . a man needs excitement," I said.

But I couldn't stop watching Trudy, scraping the plates, piling up those dishes, never giving up a squawk.

And I felt an odd twinge somewhere deep inside.

"You know what else a man needs?" I said as we rode along the wandering trail in the late forenoon. "A man needs fresh meat, and I've got a hankering for it. Trudy's a fair cook, but my tongue's raw from salt pork. I don't care if you get us a squirrel, rabbit, or turtle." I nodded at his six-shooter. "You bring him down, I'll clean him."

"I brought along some corn bread."

Albert wasn't overly concerned with my wants. He'd been hatching an odd plan ever since folding out of last night's card game. He was spontaneous as a dust devil, unpredictable as horseflies. He went for what he wanted when he wanted it. Not before or after.

Today, he wanted to give Trudy a present.

"She's a sugarfoot, putting up with us."

"We shouldn't have left her there to tend all those horses by herself."

"I know it," he said. "Which is why I want to give her something. For all her hard work."

"She might prefer we bug out completely. Indian horses and all. Let her get back to living her life."

"Aw, don't fool yourself about Trudy. She's loves company more'n anything else."

I wondered about what he said, the memory of Sonny Clausen coming to mind.

I wondered who else she might entertain while we were gone.

And how she might go about entertaining.

It was a dirty, rotten idea, and I felt like a heel for having it. But it stuck in my mind like a black walnut, and no matter how

I tried to think about something else, it crouched inside me, spreading its dark stain all over my happy mood.

Other than the obvious smearing of her virtue, I didn't know at the time why Trudy being around other men bothered me.

Naturally, I was in love with her.

I know it now. I couldn't see it then.

When Albert and I cleared the last set of rolling hills to the north, the high plains opened up around us. We rode side by side, me on my roan, Albert on a black and white pinto he picked out of the corrals. The horse was steady and nimble, a real courser. I can't deny I was jealous of it.

Watching the Kid riding high on the horizon, prancing along into the rising sun, I guess I said what I did next because I wanted to cut him down some.

My best friend in all the world, but right then I had the urge to knock out his pins.

"Trudy's not really your cousin, is she?"

Albert scrunched up his face. "You're teasing me, now, Gus."

"What's to tease? It's a yes or no question."

"You know what? No lie—I've got kin all over the Niobrara country."

"But Trudy ain't one of them."

"Oh, so? You know so much all of a sudden?"

"Just tell me the truth, we'll leave it alone."

"The truth is what I said."

"Her last name is Haas," I said. "Trudy Haas. I saw it yesterday on a bill of sale she wrote up for the Randolphs."

"Haas is a name on my mother's side."

I snorted.

Al snorted back. "Do some ciphering on this, burr-head. I've snoozed in the barn beside you the last two nights," said Al. "Do you think if Trudy wasn't my cousin, you could've held me back from paying her a visit? From spending all night long with her?"

"Maybe Moses McGee wouldn't let you."

"McGee's worthless as tits on a boar."

But saying it, he'd called my bluff. I heard it in his voice, sure, but saw it more clearly on his face. His sandy brows were arched in defiance. His jaw set off at an angle in granite.

He was daring me to confront him with any more half-baked truths.

I wondered if it was worth pressing him.

Then I wondered why any of it mattered.

If Slippery Jack wanted to play a little slap and tickle with Trudy, it wasn't my business now, was it?

"Hell, just forget it."

"You got a candle lit for her, boy?"

"Let's leave it alone."

"You damn sheepherder." Then he said, "Tell you what. We'll get her this present, and you can put your name in on it with me. It'll be from the both of us."

"You still haven't told me what you've got in mind."

"You'll see. Trudy's gonna love it. She always loves a present."

"Like the pump your old man put in?"

"Like the pump, sure. Only we're gonna give her something better."

"How much money did you get from Otto Randolph for the piebald?"

He reached up to his shirt pocket and, pulling out a roll of paper money, peeled off five bills. He handed over the money.

"Figure this is your share of the piebald. But we ain't gonna use money for Trudy's present."

"I don't understand."

"You will."

I tucked the cash into my trousers pocket.

"How'd she end up out there to Pleasant Valley all by herself? Trudy, I mean."

"Got set up with the wrong fella. Some drummer whose attention ran hot for a season. The kind of man who can't be pegged down in one spot. Like you and me, I s'pose."

"The drummer . . . he's gone now? Left the country?"

"I've seen him around."

"Maybe I know him. What's his name?"

Albert cranked his legs up to his horse's back without answering. While I watched he slapped a bare foot to his critter's spine and made as if to stand up. "Watch this," he said. "I'm King Albert riding over the Roman empire."

But the horse wouldn't quit squirming, and Al couldn't quite get to his feet.

So he settled for switching around and riding backwards for a while, mischief painted all over his face. He sure could make me laugh.

But he never told me about that drummer.

We continued to ride over fields of grass stretching forever ahead of us toward a horizon where bands of silver and olive green mixed with gold to touch the cloud-dappled sky. Our horses zigzagged through fields of prairie dog humps and shied from the shadows of buzzard wings.

We watched for rattlers and jackrabbits, Al keeping his little pistol in its holster, but always at the ready. Once we saw a clump of antelope grazing their way down a far hillside. When my roan nickered, the pronghorns picked up their heads as if of one mind and, spinning on hooves of quicksilver, drained away into a prickly canyon.

Midafternoon, Albert led us across one of the ten million cricks that dumped their meager cups into the Running Water, and we clopped around a shady grove to a white frame house tucked deep inside the trees. If you didn't know it was there, you'd never be able to find it.

The house was tall, two stories peeking over an orchard of shrubs and mulberry trees, and all the trails leading up to the front door. The ground was dirtied with black splotches and purple bird poop, and the grass was ragged and brown. Sunlight was halved in the shadowy clearing, and the temperature dropped enough to rise goose pimples on my arms.

Whitewashed wood siding in rough repair and crooked coal-black shutters gave the place a once-formal look, now on hard times.

"Land sakes, Al—is this place a funeral parlor?"

Because it looked for all the world like the last refuge of a soul's earthly plight.

As a blonde woman dressed in a long white petticoat with short sleeves padded out the front door, I realized I wasn't far from the truth.

But Al barked loud at my question, tossing his reins away to slide from the piebald onto his squishy spurred boots. "How do, Squeaky?"

Squeaky was everything Trudy wasn't. Loud and brash. Thick and puffy like fried doughnuts—with the same kind of oily rough hide. Her overgrown, powdered hair strained at a hunk of yarn in back, yearning to be free. She smelled of lard and lye soap, had a ponderous big chest with a belted waist, and wore bedroom slippers outside.

Kid Wade knew her well enough to lead with his lips.

Again.

"You're fulla spunk today, Kid."

"Guess I ain't alone, Squeaky. This here's August John."

Squeaky wagged her eyelashes and put a purr into her voice. "Lovely meeting you, John."

"Most folks call me Gus."

"Gus it is," she agreed. "I'm Squeaky."

"Pretty name."

"She makes a bedspring talk, this one does," Al said.

Squeaky slapped his shoulder.

Al's head was on a busy swivel. "Don't look like nobody's around."

"Just me and Cinnamon," Squeaky said, "and she's sleepin' upstairs. You want me to wake her up?"

"Naw, don't bother about it. Where's Heavy?"

"Mr. Frahm rode to town for supplies. I imagine he'll be along shortly."

"Should oughta work okay," Albert said.

"Plenty of playtime left," Squeaky said, wrapping her arms around Al's waist like twin snakes, only to slide from him to me.

She bumped my hat back with her own forehead as she laced her hands behind my neck. Just like that, she planted a big ol' kiss smack dab on my mouth, drawing her tongue along my top lip.

"F'r crying out loud, lady." I stumbled backwards beside my horse, nearly plopping over into the dirt. I swear, she was old enough to be my mother. And her tongue's what scared me.

But she had nice, white teeth.

Squeaky doubled over laughing like a drunk mule, her hair finally spilling from the ribbon to drop all over her shoulders and hang down across her face. "Ain't you a sight, August John."

"You might give a fellow some warning." I picked up my hat and dusted myself off.

"Gus ain't never been with a gal."

I shot Al the stink eye, the rotten skunk. "I been with lots of gals."

Squeaky arched her eyebrows, a smirk of amusement traveling like an electric current from her green eyes to her twitching rosy cheeks to her half-parted lips and back around. "Do tell?"

I swatted the dust from my britches with my hat and jammed it back on my head.

"Gentlemen don't kiss and tell, ma'am, and I happen to be a gentleman."

Squeaky stood up tall and aligned her shoulders proper. "Oh, my heavens. To be in the presence of a gentleman." She winked at me and said, "We won't hold it against you, sir."

Then she dropped an arm over Al's shoulder, going from being all playful, to all business. "You ready to come inside?" She cocked her head, saying to me, "Does the gentleman want to join us?"

I replied with as much Christian piety as I could dig up. "I 'spect somebody ought to be here to greet this . . . uh, Mr. Frahm upon his return."

"Shucks, Squeaky, we ain't here for none of what you're selling," said Al.

Squeaky seemed hurt and slunk away almost like Al had given her a shove. "You ain't, huh? Then what *are* you pony boys here for?"

I was wondering the same thing myself.

Which one of us was more surprised by Al's answer, I can't say.

"We're here for your fainting couch."

"Say again?"

Albert put his hand to his holster like a rough outlaw. "We're taking your fainting couch home with us. It's gonna be a present for a friend of ours."

"I don't think our fainting couch is for sale."

"Doesn't matter if it is or not. We're taking it. Free of charge."

As far as Kid Wade's wild schemes went, this was a corker.

Squeaky couldn't hold back her laughter. "Albert Wade, you sorry bastard." She slapped his chest and backed off again with a series of snickers. "You had me there for a minute. Stealing my fainting couch."

"I ain't kidding, Squeaky."

"He's kidding," I said.

"No, I ain't, Gus."

"Well, criminy, Al—how're we gonna carry a fainting couch all the way back to— ?"

"Shht."

"Back to . . . our friend?"

"Figured we would borrow one of Heavy Frahm's wagons."

Squeaky snickered again. "Now you're gonna steal a wagon? You're out of your damn mind, Albert."

"I told you so on more than one occasion." He winked. "But you never believed me."

"Heavy'll pound your ass to pork sausage, you lift one of his wagons."

"Not if you don't tell him it was us who took it."

Squeaky saw an opportunity, and she circled Al like a friendly kitten, rubbing herself against him. "What'll you give me to keep quiet?"

Al bared his lips, talking through clenched teeth. "A smack in the mouth if you don't?"

Squeaky lifted her chin and kissed Al on the cheek. "God, I love you," she said. Then, biting her bottom lip with her front two teeth, she said, "Are you really gonna steal the couch?"

"I'm really gonna."

Squeaky giggled and pranced toward the front door like a gleeful kid playing a schoolyard game. "Follow me."

At the threshold, Al turned around to look at me. "Ain't you coming?"

Chapter Six

The fainting couch was roughly four and a half feet long, less than two feet wide, and the back was an ornamental piece of wood carved up with lions and tigers and some kind of flowers I've never seen before.

Stuffed with straw and upholstered with red velvet and brass tacks, it sat on four stubby legs, six inches off the floor, and weighed near on a hundred pounds.

"It's beautiful. Tell me Trudy ain't gonna love it, Gus?"

"I can't imagine . . ."

"Can't imagine what?"

"I can't imagine she wouldn't love it."

"It's what she's always wanted, and it will go well with the dining table. I mean, you see what she has to sit on—those sorry hack-job stools."

I tried to imagine pulling up to my supper plate from the fainting couch, but I knew what he was aiming at. I guess his heart was more or less in the right place for a change.

"It will certainly add some color to the place," I said.

"Sure it will." He popped his knuckles. "Now . . . do you figure two rough and tumble gents like us can get 'er hoisted out of here?"

"It's not so much the weight," I said, giving the couch a nudge with the toe of my boot. "But threading the damn thing out of here."

Because only the good Lord knew how anybody ever got it

parked where it was.

Heavy Frahm's cathouse was built around an enclosed central staircase. When we walked in the front door, we might've turned left into a wallpapered parlor or to the right into a kitchen stinking of cooked cabbage and onions.

Instead, we stayed in the narrow hallway, not too wide, which led on the left to the back door. On the right, Squeaky took Albert by the hand and up a steep flight of rickety steps. I followed to a narrow landing on the second floor. Here, we turned and doubled back along a railed hallway to the upstairs rooms.

The hardwood floor was unfinished, and the boards squalled and complained like a chorus of milk-starved calves.

The second-story rooms were closed off for business with solid six-paneled doors, so the hall was dark and shadowy.

Everything smelled of week-old sour cooking and stale cigar smoke.

I took in the closed doors and without thinking where I was said, "Al, you ever heard of the door bible?" He looked at me like I was off my feed, so I traced the two square recessed flat panels up top and the two taller panels below. "See here how the door makes a cross?" Then, kicking lightly at the two lower panels, explained, "These two down here are the open pages of the Good Book."

"Not just a gentleman, now he's a preacher?" Squeaky said.

Al gave me a good frown and moved on. "Ignore him."

We found the fainting couch jammed in at the end of the hall, up against the front outside wall of the house.

The space was just wide enough to accommodate the furniture without an inch to spare on either end.

Overtop the ornamental backrest was a grand landscape painting of a naked woman covered with fruit.

"Pretty rich looking, huh, Gus?"

"Pears and apples and grapes I recognize." The rest of the

painting would require more study. I scratched my chin, pondering every brushstroke.

Squeaky giggled, and Al hit me with his hat. "I'm talking about the daybed, thistle-head."

By now the girl named Cinnamon—whom Squeaky called Sin—had joined us, appearing from one of the rooms like a ghost. She had silky, long red hair with a plank body and boney arms.

Her long, white slip dragged on the floor, and I could see right away she wasn't wearing any pears or grapes or anything underneath.

As far as girls go, Sin looked more like my own stick drawing than the subject of the fruit painting on the wall.

A brown glass bottle, half full of a dark liquid, sat on the floor in front of the daybed. Sin picked it up and put it to her lips. With hooded eyes, she passed it to me. "I'm Sin," she said.

"I think I know you from Sunday school," I said.

Nobody laughed at my joke, so I passed the bottle to Squeaky without drinking and clapped Al on the shoulder. "How about we bring Trudy a bunch of wildflowers instead?"

"I think if we both lift, we can carry it to the lip of the steps."

Bending at the waist, I scootched the couch forward a few inches away from the cracked plaster wall.

"You're sure we can't do wildflowers?"

Sin suddenly understood Al's intent and dropped her jaw. "They're taking our couch?"

"Stealing it," Squeaky said under a wrinkled nose. "Ain't it a laugh? What a joke on Heavy. I can't wait to see his face."

"But . . . but why?" Sin planted her hands on her hard hip bones. "Why are you stealing our couch?"

"This here is Kid Wade," said Squeaky. "And August John."

Like it explained everything.

I guess in some ways it did.

"You all work for Doc Middleton, don't you?" Sin said. "What's he like?"

Squeaky shushed her. "You know what he's like. I've told you all about ol' Doc."

"You know Doc?" I said.

"Couple years ago, we had a girl staying with us named Louise. Wouldn't you know, one day ol' Lou falls pregnant. So Heavy lets her stay until her time comes, and the day it does, it happens Doc is here, payin' us a visit."

"Don't tell me he delivered the baby, because we both know Jim Middleton isn't a true-to-life bona fide doctor."

At least I hope she knew it, because some people believed James C. Riley, aka Jim Middleton, aka Doc, was a real-life sawbones. Where his nickname came from is anybody's guess, but Doc once said it was laid on him for being a good horse doctor, but somebody else said it was for his skill at doctoring brands.

"I know he's not a physician," said Squeaky, "but he rode three hours one way and three hours back to bring one when Louise had trouble. Doc Middleton saved her baby's life. Probably saved Louise. Without the help of Middleton, there would've been no doctor here to help."

Sin nodded in agreement. "I've heard lots of stories about how he helps people."

I didn't think I ought to tell 'em what we heard about Doc—the idea he was most likely dead and buried out west someplace.

Albert ignored both girls. "Here, Gus, let me get on one end. You get on the other."

There was no space between the end of the couch and the wall, so again I scooted the front out until we had the thing at an angle. With a couple more moves, we had it resting in the middle of the hallway, almost parallel with the walls, and Al could get between the far end and the fruity painting on the wall.

"Let's get it to the steps," said Al, bending over.

I wrapped my fingers under the slender wood frame between the front and back legs, busting through strands of sticky spiderweb, feeling the skitter of little legs prance away.

Letting out a whoosh of air, I stood up.

Al did the same, and we had the couch balanced in the air between us.

"Now what?"

"Carry it, carry it."

Al drove forward, and I stumbled backwards four steps, carrying my end of the couch into the space between wall and stairwell railing.

"There's no room to turn it onto the landing," I said, because to position the couch perpendicular to the steps would mean no room on either side for me or Albert.

"We'll have to go over the railing. You lift your end up and set it there. Then go around into the stairwell, and I'll turn my end and push it over."

"What am I supposed to do?"

"You're gonna catch it and lower it into the stairwell."

"And how am I supposed to hold the weight all by myself?"

Al glanced at the two girls. "You wanna help him?"

"Oh, no," said Squeaky. "Bad back. I can't lift a thing."

Albert harrumphed. " 'Bad back.' "

"Hazard of the business," I said.

"Kiss my ass," said Squeaky.

"What's the going rate?"

She broke out into her horsey laugh. "You couldn't afford it." From somewhere, she had produced a sack of tobacco leaves and rolling paper.

Casually, she built a smoke while I stood there stretching out my arms. "I don't want to be the one standing underneath that furniture when you drop it on me."

"I ain't gonna drop it on you," Al said. "I'm stronger than you think."

"I don't know."

"Cryin' out loud, will you just lift it up to the rail?"

What else could I do?

I put some effort into it and did what he asked, dropping the couch frame onto the rail with a crunch. It swayed back and forth under the weight.

"Now go down a few steps and catch it when I push it over," said Al.

"I think the railing's gonna bust," I said.

As if to prove my point, the end post creaked like a bobcat.

Albert shoved the couch out over the abyss. "Grab hold, Gus."

I went down three steps, put my arms in the air, caught hold of the end of the couch . . .

For two or three seconds I stood rock solid.

I was a bridge pillar. A wall stud. A barn stanchion.

Al shoved again, and the entire weight of the couch landed on me.

I was a buckling whipsaw.

As the weight came over to my side of the railing, I let go, stepped back, and flattened myself against the wall.

The fainting couch toppled into the stairwell.

My end thudded down onto the fourth stair, and I lurched sideways. Albert's end crashed into the sidewall, hooking a stub leg into the plaster, missing my head by two inches.

The couch hung suspended in the stairway by one corner, whining, uncertain, like a dog diving into the creek on a hot summer day. When the plaster let go, the overturned daybed pitched into a tumultuous slide to the bottom.

The final, jarring impact knocked the backrest free and splintered the frame.

"Hells bells," said Albert, rushing past.

"You might at least ask me if I'm all right."

"Are you all right?" said Squeaky.

"I think you broke the railing," said Sin.

Alone in the stairwell, I saw she was right. When the couch fell, its weight pulled the stair railing over with it, snapping the spindles and top post at floor level.

"Easy enough to fix," I said, trying to sound confident as I imagined Heavy Frahm coming home to find us tearing up his house.

I shuddered, my fear compounded by the fact I had never laid eyes on the man in my life.

What kind of ape ran a whorehouse and called himself *Heavy*?

"You think we maybe oughta just leave, Al?"

Albert was busy tugging on the backrest of the couch, trying to free the final nail from the upholstered frame. "I. *Tug.* Ain't. *Tug.* Leavin'. *Tug.* Without. *Tug.* The. *Tug.* Couch."

When the square-headed nail broke free of the soft wood frame, Al went over onto his backside with a curse.

Much to Squeaky and Sin's delight.

I hurried down the stairs to help him up. "Are you okay?"

Back on his feet, Al kicked the poor couch's broken seat. "Damn thing just wants to be cantankerous."

"Stop horsing around, Al. The couch is wrecked. Forget it."

But Al had already turned his violence against the backrest, grabbing ahold with both hands. Hauling it up to waist level, he hurled it toward the entrance to the house, where it smashed into the door jamb.

"See what I mean? See what I mean? Cantankerous!"

He followed up on his pitch with another series of oaths and wild swings at the furniture with his boot. Tacks popped high into the air as the soft upholstery let go. Dust and yellow straw spilled out onto the floor.

"This thing is nothing but junk!"

Once his immediate temper was spent, I slid the backrest across the floor, out of the way, and went to the couch frame.

"Help me get the seat through the door."

Squeaky sneezed, and Al bellowed, "What are you laughing at?"

"She ain't laughing, Kid," I said.

"She better not be."

I tossed off a warning look toward the girls and picked up my end of the couch bottom and drug it backwards several inches along the floor. "Let's get this part outside, then."

Albert gripped his end by the corners and stomped toward me, shoving the unwieldy couch between us toward the door. At the threshold, I said, "Hang on a second." But naturally he didn't.

The wood frame was a couple inches wider than the door. We hammered it with a resounding thump, shaking the entire front of the house.

The fat impact jarred Al and caught my fingers between door jamb and couch.

I yelled, dropped my burden, and backpedaled out the door.

Full of steam and half-blind with frustration, Al took two steps backwards, pulled his pistol, and emptied the entire cylinder into the daybed, tearing the upholstery to ribbons and splintering the already wounded frame.

Echoes of the Colt's six explosions bounced off the trees.

Al kicked aside a piece of debris and marched outside.

Squeaky and Sin stood over the remains of the couch like it was wounded game.

"Let's get out of here," Al said.

"What about the couch?"

"It's worthless now. Just leave it."

Leaving it was a good idea, but I felt bad for the girls.

"Are you two gonna be all right?"

Squeaky waved me on. "Go on, get out of here before Heavy gets home."

She said it again, but Al was already on his piebald, spinning up some dust.

"I've got some money," I said, reaching up to my shirt pocket. "Let me pay you for the couch."

"Forget it," said Squeaky. "You just get while you still can."

She flicked the remnants of her cigarette to the ground and stepped on it.

I guess none of it was funny anymore.

I held up my hand in farewell and climbed into my saddle.

Halfway out the lane, Sin hollered my name and ran to catch up.

"You'll come back, won't you?"

"Aw, heck." I looked around the sun-dappled place, then shook my head. "Guess it's pretty unlikely, ma'am."

"You sure? I like you, August John. Don't you like me?"

"I don't have anything against you."

"Remember when you said you knew me from Sunday school?"

"I do."

She pulled her top down and bared her breasts. "I never been to Sunday school," she said.

"I reckon you ain't," I said.

I couldn't think of anything else to say, so I turned to catch up with Albert.

No man ever rode away from sin so fast.

By the time Kid Wade and I were halfway back to Pleasant Valley, neither one of us had said a word, but I could tell he'd cooled off some.

We topped a pair of rolling hills, and Al turned crossways with the sunset when I spoke to him.

"Do you like them two? Back at the cathouse, I mean. Do you think they're pretty?"

"I guess I like 'em okay."

"But are they pretty?"

"I suppose so. Who cares?"

"The one called Cinnamon? I think I like her better with her clothes on."

"Are you touched in the head or something? And what was all the talk about the door being like a bible?"

I wasn't sure what I meant by any of it, so we rode a while more, and Al said, "Trudy would've loved the fainting couch."

"She won't ever know one way or the other."

"Goddamn Heavy Frahm's a cheap bastard. Buying second-rate furniture. Did you see how the damn thing fell apart soon as we touched it?"

I had never met Heavy Frahm in person, but the name conjured up a hulking despot who snapped bones like dry kindling.

"I hope he doesn't take it out on Squeaky and Sin."

"Take what out?"

"A man comes home to find his place wrecked, he might be upset."

"He probably comes home to something like it every day."

"I hope he's not as quick to temper as you."

"So what if he is?"

"I hope he doesn't have a gun."

"You need to toughen up, Gus. You're starting to sound like—"

"A damned sheepherder, I know."

His laughing broke the tension for a few minutes, but we

continued to ride along in silence, the afternoon turning to evening, the evening turning to deeper shadows.

Less than two miles from Pleasant Valley we took a short cut through an open grove of locust and oak trees, the woods thick and smelling of mildew and rotting groundcover.

And then stinking of rotting flesh.

We found the two men hanged from the sturdy boughs of an enormous oak tree, the wood creaking as it moved in the night's breeze, the stretched hemp singing with vibration.

The cadavers were bloated, vile looking things, staring at Al and me with bulging, accusatory eyes.

You can always tell a horse thief by the way he swings a rope.

It was Windy Barnes and Boots Harper, as croaked as if Kid Wade had shot them with his pistol the first night on Holt Creek.

As far as the twenty horses they stole from us, there was no sign.

Chapter Seven

Never was a man resurrected so wonderfully glorious as Doc Middleton when he thundered into Pleasant Valley the next morning on a chestnut gelding with Curley Grimes and Jack Nolan flanking each side, carbines held high, on lightning-swift black mares.

Blustery and humid, it was like Doc himself whipped up the storm clouds in the west, thick and rich and a deep blue-black. The tattered horizon was crimson red over the sunrise in the east. I was just shuffling from the barn barefoot without a shirt and bleary-eyed through a passel of chickens when the three of them landed.

I hadn't slept good the night before, having found Boots and Windy on our way home. Their damn stinking smell of rot stuck in my nose, and me wondering who might've strung 'em up such a way and why.

Albert and I cut them down and let 'em rest in the grass of the cottonwood grove under some piled up brush until we could think what to do.

Now with our early morning company, we had that much more to consider.

Curley and Jack Nolan spun their horses in a circle before coming to rest, and Doc paraded between, face held up to the sky like royalty, his yard-long beard pouring down his shirt like a waterfall and tucked into his waistband at the belt buckle.

They were Lucifer and his devil ranch hands cast from

heaven, and they were magnificent.

"The hell if it ain't Doc," I said out loud. And then louder, to get Kid Wade's attention. "Shoot-fire, Al, get yourself out here right away! It's Doc Middleton and his boys."

More than six feet tall, with wide shoulders and slender at the waist, Doc swung down from the saddle in a flurry of dust like he didn't see me, covering the space to Trudy's front door with three long strides.

Maybe Doc didn't see me, but Curley Grimes and Jack Nolan sure did.

They reminded me of the old Roman sentries I seen in a book once, all stuck-up and full of themselves behind their pointy noses and long guns. Curley and Jack Nolan, I mean. The Romans had long spears.

Doc stopped at the front of the house and started banging a racket at the door.

"Halooo, the house. Come on, open up!"

Al had jumped into some trousers and had a shirt draped over his shoulders when he came dancing out on one foot, struggling to pull on his other boot. "What's all this about Doc?"

He couldn't help but stare straight at Curley and Jack, them towering over us evil-eyed on their huffing mounts. Curley turned to look at Albert and gave him this crummy smirk, like Al wasn't worth the time of day.

I wasn't having it, so I walked right up to him and said, "How-do, Grimes?" I nodded at Jack, then addressed Curley again, "Heard you boys had some trouble out Sidney-way."

He carried a scar on his neck from a Ponca squaw who tried to kill him in his sleep. His hands were knobby and wrinkled and showed his true age more than his smooth-shaved face. I think he was older even than Doc. He wore a hog-iron on his hip, and some folks called him the fastest gun west of the Missouri. With those big hands of his, I was skeptical.

Curley didn't say a word, just looked down on me like a man looks at a bug on a hot summer's day while he thinks about squishing it.

Nolan, a few years older than me, but not as old as Curley, acted the same.

I sniffed like it didn't matter to me either way.

Both of them boys were bad apples, and I wish'd Doc wouldn't let 'em follow along with him. Curley sometimes went by the name of Lee Grimes and other times he was Lew Curley. He was from Texas, just like Joe Smith, another man who rode with Doc. And Nolan had been in jail, accused of killing a Mexican.

I guess Al figured I had Curley and Jack in hand, so as soon as he fell forward into his boot, he went tearing across the yard like his pants was on fire. "Good Lord, Doc," he said. "Goddammit, man, we heard you'd been killed."

Trudy had yet to open the door to the house, so Doc used the time to turn casually toward Kid Wade.

Folks nowadays would have you believe these two notorious Nebraska owlhoots were chums of long standing, and it's true there was something between 'em.

But whatever it was, I never quite figured it out.

Some folks said Albert worshipped Doc like a puppy at his master's heels, and it ain't true at all. Them same people will tell you Doc hardly knew Al or treated him with contempt. And it ain't true either.

They weren't friends, but they weren't not friends.

Like everything in the world, it was more complicated than people had time or effort to worry about. Worries take time, and most folks out West, especially back then, didn't have a lot of time allotted to 'em for worrying about things that weren't their business.

Me, I think Doc saw himself in Kid Wade—the rascal and the

Samaritan both. I think it was in Albert he clearly saw the fork in the road, one way leading to a good family life, one way pitching straight at the gallows. I ain't saying I saw it at the time, and I ain't saying Doc tried to push Albert one way or the other—most times Doc wasn't sure himself which direction he rode.

In any case, Al's fate was soon to be sealed, though none of us knew it.

Whatever Doc truly thought about Al, he greeted him at Pleasant Valley like a little brother—with grudging good humor and a touch of menace.

"Land sakes, if it ain't the Kid," Doc said, clamping a big hand around the back of Al's neck and giving him a shake. "Kinda thought I'd find you here. In fact, I was counting on it."

Oblivious to Doc's ominous tone, the reunion meant a lot to Al, and in between slapping Doc's shoulders and gripping his arms, he yapped like a schoolgirl. "Jesus, it's good to see you. Real good to see you, sure."

I half expected the boy was gonna wrap his arms around the tall man and bury his face in the beard.

The whiskers were long, but Doc's hair was short on the sides with a curled shock of ebony combed fancy over his forehead. His mustache was clipped straight with his lip, the affectation of a banker, lawyer, or business tycoon. Not yet thirty years old, with clear eyes under perpetually amused eyebrows, he spoke soft and rare around his famous gold tooth.

Dwarfed by Doc's stature, almost homely next to Doc's pretty peach skin, Al couldn't shut up.

"But what are you doing around here? Shucks, we heard you was killed, Doc. What happened out to Sidney?"

Curley and Jack sidled up closer to the house, and I followed along with them.

Before Doc could answer Kid Wade, Curley spoke with a

voice coming from a hollow, dank spot inside his chest. "A man said there was Indian horses out this way. Maybe a whole lot of Indian horses. Thought we'd come take a look-see."

Al stepped up to Curley's horse and then turned his head back toward Doc. "Well, it's true, Doc. You see them trotters over there in the corrals? We just brung them in from the Pine Ridge, me and Gus and Dill Schiller. I guess maybe Dill caught up with you? I sent him out personal to find you, Doc. Let you know."

"Ain't seen Dill Schiller," said Curley.

Out of the blue, and without thinking, I said, "By chance, maybe you've seen Boots Harper or Windy Barnes?" Them two had stayed firm in the back of my mind—and my nose.

Curley's eyes were cold chips of iron.

It was the wrong thing to say, and I wondered if they knew about the hangings or not.

"We ain't seen anybody," said Jack Nolan. "We like it that way."

"But what happened in Sidney, Doc?" Al said. "You gotta know we were all kinds of worried."

"Joe Smith is dead," said Curley.

Al put his hand on his chest for dramatic affect. "Heavens to Betsy."

It was true—one of Doc's party had been killed just as Otto Randolph heard.

It was no surprise the news had twisted its way through the local sausage grinder and come out as if Doc himself were the victim. Damn, I was glad it wasn't Doc had been killed.

But Joe hadn't been a bad egg, and the news was pitiful sad.

"You knew Joe, didn't you, Gus?"

"I knew him some, just to say hello. What happened?"

"Doc tells it," said Curley. "We weren't there, were we, Jack?"

"Nothing much to tell," said Doc. "I wasn't there either, not at the killing. Some law boys from North Platte were laying for us. Joe fell for one of them, got lured into an ambush. Then they came hell-for-leather across the prairie for me. I made it home okay."

"Yeah, but Joe . . . dead," Albert said.

You could tell he didn't really care, he was just showing off.

Albert hadn't been close to Joe.

Doc brushed the topic away like shooing flies. "Anyway, I'm glad to find you boys here."

Al toed the dirt, and the silence went on too long and turned uncomfortable.

The space between all of us felt awkward and pregnant with something that wasn't being said out loud. An accusation, maybe a reckoning about the Indian horses and us hiding them here in Pleasant Valley.

Windy and Boots swaying in the night breeze swept through my mind, and I shivered.

Every now and then Doc would flick his gaze away from Al and up toward Curley or Jack.

He never looked at me.

"You ain't here by yourself, Al?" he said. "Where's the mistress of the house?"

"Mistress? Oh, you mean Trudy."

"I guess I mean Trudy."

"What'd you want her for?"

"What do you think?"

Al hesitated before answering. "I guess I ain't sure."

Curley said, "We're lookin' for a breakfast. Eggs, ham, toast."

Jack nodded. "Sonny Clausen says Trudy makes the best breakfast this side of Sugarloaf Hill."

"I figured you had talked to Clausen," Al said. "He's the one who told you about the Indian ponies, ain't he?"

A comment that seemed only to stoke the fire of the steam

cooker between us all.

"Clausen's not wrong about Trudy's breakfast," I said. "I'll get us some eggs."

I turned around and moseyed back past the chickens into the barn, real careful and nonchalant.

It was all I could do not to run. Turning my back on the pressure, I liked to have shot into the barn like a hot rivet spit from the side of a boiling locomotive.

But, be damned, I wouldn't let them see me shake.

The blustering storm clouds flattened out while we talked, falling over the dome of morning sky like a gray paper shade, covering the sun. Our three visitors were the same, pulling a cloak of darkness behind them so it drifted down to cover me like a shroud.

First Boots and Windy, then the news about Joe, and now the unspoken something hanging between us and Doc's men. The whole sorrowful package had me jittery.

Collecting the eggs in a pail, I broke three before finally having enough to carry inside. Trudy was more'n happy to make breakfast and put on a spread like I never saw from her before. Eggs, toast. Gravy and fried taters, pork and beans.

The King had arrived, and the reason it took so long to answer the door was clear in the powder and rouge on Trudy's cheeks.

She ignored my comment.

I carried an iron skillet back to the cookstove and swapped it out for a tall coffeepot. "This is some kind of chow. You been holding out on us, Trudy-beauty."

"There's fresh cream for your coffee, boys," she told the room, shoving a small tin pouring pitcher into my free hand.

"Fresh cream?" said Jack Nolan. "I do declare, I ain't ever seen such service." Atop one of the three stools, he moved his head around to watch each of us. "You fellas ever seen such a gal?" Nolan wore his flat-brimmed black hat all through the meal, and his gun hung low from his belt and banged against the legs of his short stool. It was an old single-action Remmy.

The room smelled salty and tart in the back of my throat, and steam from the coffee whirled around like it does when bacon is fried in shadowy blue window light.

Rumbles came from high above, but it had yet to rain.

Seated at the dining table on the other side of Nolan, Doc held up his tin cup while I filled it.

"It is indeed an awfully fine meal. Can I help with the dishes, Trudy?"

"Of course not," she said.

"You'll let us pay for the hospitality?"

Trudy put her hand on her hip in mock indignation. "Most certainly not. I swear, Mr. Middleton."

"Call me Jim," he said. Doc's real name was James Riley, but nobody ever said it.

"I swear," Trudy said as Doc slipped a dime under his plate.

It was a game. Nobody showing their true face, their real emotion. Everything was playacting.

Me, too.

I poured coffee for the other two seated men, then returned the pot to its cast-iron place on the stove.

Out of the blue, Doc turned to me. "You said something to Curley about Boots Harper?"

Good thing I'd already let go of the pot, or I'd have dropped it right there.

"I did?"

I guess Doc had been listening before when I was talking to Curley. Listening more closely than I reckoned. Doc noticed everything. Even when it seemed like he wasn't paying attention, he was.

If he was listening now, he'd hear the tremor in my voice.

"W-what about Boots?"

"You asked if we had seen Boots and Windy. Why did you want to know?"

Hemmed in, I figured I might as well tell him. When I did, it gushed out of me honest.

"Boots and Windy were riding with us. They helped bring in them Indian horses. Then they left us alone partway between here and there."

Doc narrowed his eyes and nodded slow, like he was chewing on every morsel I gave him.

"You know they had some other horses with 'em," he said. "Buckskins with notched ears don't come from the Pine Ridge Agency."

How did he know?

"If it's so, I wasn't aware of it," I said. So much for being honest.

"It's a matter of fact."

The back of my throat was dry, and I picked up a tin cup from a little table beside Trudy's stove. "Oh, them horses must've come from someplace else," I said.

I had never, ever been afraid of Doc. Until then. For some reason, my heart was beating a bass drum.

"You don't know where the horses came from?" Doc said.

I gripped the handle of the coffeepot and held my nerves steady.

It helped I could tell the truth.

"I don't know where they came from." Albert had never told me.

I tipped the pot, and it was a miracle every drop I poured managed to land in the cup. Doc turned his attention away from me.

"How about you, Kid? You know where them notch-ears came from?"

Al wasn't gonna be bullied, and he fed it right back to Doc.

"I'd like to know how you know about them? It sure sounds like you've been talking to Dill Schiller."

"It's not your business who we talk to," Curley said. "How about you answer the man's question?"

Al cleared his throat, then spoke straight to Doc's face. "Fact is, I found 'em wandering along the trail."

Doc sipped his coffee. "Along the trail, west of Holt Crick?"

"Yep. Right there west of Holt Crick."

"The notches didn't mean anything to you?"

Jack Nolan spoke up. "I once had a horse with notches like it. Prize horse name of White Flanks."

Doc chuckled once, deep in his throat. "You had a horse. You mean you thieved a horse," he said. Then to Albert, "White Flanks belonged to Print Olive. Along them same lines, I wonder if you found them buckskins wandering on the trail near somebody's ranch? Maybe Otto Randolph's?"

Al's cheeks spread out wide. "That's as may be," he said.

"I made Nolan take White Flanks back home."

"Yeah?"

Doc pursed his lips, slow to answer. "Yeah," he said.

"How come?"

I didn't like how the look on Doc's face had gone from overall funnin' to smokey perturbed. Now he was chewing on the inside of his bottom lip and turning his coffee cup in circles on the table.

Albert's eyes went from the cup to Doc, back to the cup. He chuckled. "How come you made him take the horse back?"

Doc's fingers were tight around the cup, knuckles blazing white.

"How come, Doc?"

An explosion of hot coffee hit Albert's face, and Doc leaped from the stool to grip his collar. He slammed Al into the side of the house, and one of Trudy's plates slipped off the counter, landing with a crash of forks and knives.

Doc lashed out at Al with a hollering torrent. "I made him take it back because stealing it from Mr. Olive was an asinine thing to do. Just like you stealing from Mr. Randolph was a stupid thing to do."

Doc's big claws were hooked into the material of Al's shirt, scrunching it around his neck into a noose. "Do you understand me? Can you comprehend what I am trying to say?"

"I . . . I ain't sure."

Doc slammed Al into the wall again, and this time his head thumped hard enough against the wood, we could hear it.

"A dog ought not do his dirty business in his own backyard. I thought you knew it."

"I thought . . ."

"You didn't think. You never goddamn think." Doc was close up in Al's face now, each word spraying spit and curses. "The Randolphs are our neighbors. Sure as Trudy here's our neighbor, or Mr. Clausen. You gonna steal from Trudy next? Maybe steal away Mr. Randolph's new piebald?"

Doc loosened his grip so Al could answer.

"It was me sold Randolph the piebald."

Gleefully watching the ordeal, Curley Grimes couldn't help but contribute. "Hell, we know you did, Wade. We just figure you're dumb enough to steal it back."

"Damn Dill Schiller can't keep his mouth shut," Al said.

Doc's muscles bulged, and he near lifted Al off the floor.

"Nobody shits in my backyard, Kid. Nobody."

"I never meant nothing bad toward you, Doc."

"You damn right you didn't." He pushed Al backwards, watching him sink to the floor before striding back across to the table, where he picked up the spilled plate and utensils. Setting them back on the counter, he tipped his hat to Trudy over a flushed red forehead. “Sorry about the spectacle, ma’am. Especially first thing in the morning. I hate to get the day off to a poor start.”

Trudy bowed her head. “I understand.”

“I hope we can still do business?” Doc indicated the back room.

“Naturally.”

Doc turned back to Al and gazed at him for a full minute while catching his breath. Then he turned back to Trudy and held out his hand.

“If you’d lead the way?”

Trudy turned around and walked past the cookstove to the back of the room. She opened the door into her bedroom.

“We won’t be long,” Doc told us. Then to Curley: “Make sure your horses are ready, and take them Pony Boys out to the Indian herd. Soon as I’m square here, we’ll ride out.”

“Ride out to where?” Al said.

“Never mind where,” Jack Nolan said. “Just come along.”

“I don’t understand,” I said.

At Trudy’s door, Doc sounded tired and impatient, his cool demeanor burned away by his temper. “What’s to understand, August John? We’re taking Little Wound’s horses with us.”

Of course all the talk about a dog not messing up his backyard was supposed to be a tried and true philosophy for Doc’s gettin’ along with folks on the Running Water, but it was all horse apples.

T’was the self-assured hypocrisy only young people under a certain age can pull off.

In ’79, Doc Middleton called Albert “Kid,” but the truth was he was only a few years out of short pants himself.

Every story you get from an old-timer tells about Doc doing good for the community, like he maybe did for the gal at Heavy’s cathouse, but I can tell you otherwise.

I saw the difference between truth and storybooks firsthand, and I sure enough heard about the difference later on, after Doc was gone, and people felt like it was okay to talk about him.

Turns out, three weeks before Joe Smith was killed, on the way out to Sidney, Doc stopped at the Cottonwood Ranch and stole Phil Dufrand's horse, and a notch-ear from Randolph's place.

At least, it's what I heard later, after Llewellyn came in and shot things up and took Doc away.

After how I hurt Trudy and Al turned on me, and we all got most of what we had coming.

In Pleasant Valley it rained buckets once we had our horses saddled up and ready to go, and Curley Grimes wasn't happy to wait on anybody.

He clucked his tongue and rolled his eyes toward heaven, pouring the water off his hat every ten seconds. His head was shaved clean and shiny underneath and the Ponca scar on his neck blazed orange the more irritable Curley got.

Finally, he'd had enough, and he barked at Nolan.

"Open the damned gate, Jack. Set them bastards free."

Nolan stood soaking wet beside his black mare, holding the reins at the corral's front gate. "We're not gonna leave without Doc?"

"Did you hear me?"

The two bad men locked eyes, but it was Nolan who blinked.

"Screw it." Nolan went ahead and pulled the latch—maybe because Curley had his rifle balanced across his lap, or maybe because the rain came down harder then.

The gate fell backwards onto the ground with a *wop.*

After a few seconds, some critters slipped free and galloped toward the eastern hills. Seconds later, it was like pulling a cork from a dyke at a reservoir, the horses pouring through, tossing their heads and kicking up their hooves, flaps of mud and damp chaff flying.

All those wild animals lurching and shoving through the gate.

Albert pulled his hat tight over his head and yelled at me before sinking his spurs deep into his animal's side. "Go get Doc. Tell him we gotta go."

Kid Wade bolted one direction, and I hurried off in another.

How was I to know I wouldn't see him again for near on a month?

I pert' near broke down the front door of the station, my slippery boots sliding to a stop on the hardpan floor outside Trudy's room. The door was cracked open, and I could hear Doc and Trudy inside, talking sweet to each other.

"Oh, yeah. You've got exactly what I need, girl."

"How about this?"

"Yeah, better. Much, much better."

I shuffled my feet for a minute and scratched at my wet scalp. Swallowed hard.

Good Lord in heaven, now what should I do?

My shirt and trousers clung to my skin, making everything itch, and it seemed steamy inside the house and too cramped.

"You're going cheap, my dear," Doc said.

"It's kind of you to say so."

What a stupid place to be, I thought.

Who knows how Doc would react at being interrupted—him doing whatever he was in there doing.

Damn Albert Wade's eyes!

And who did he think he was, bossing me around all the time?

Right then, I felt the same way I'd felt riding out with Al the day before. I wanted to bowl him over with a sock to the jaw, him and his possum-head ideas. I wanted to smash his face in with the frying pan on Trudy's stove.

Him always slobbering over Doc. He was no better than Dill Schiller.

See what it gets you, I thought, turning my back to Trudy's door. See what all this running horses gets you.

For maybe the first time ever, I thought about busting away from Al and living on my own.

Then I felt an inadvertent shudder go through me. The gruesome memory of Boots and Windy spilled into mind, and I wondered if Dill Schiller was still alive.

I wondered what Doc knew about the hangings.

In what little schooling I had, I remembered some old boy said it was better to hang together than hang separate.

I thought maybe it was true. In spite of his being a pain in my backside sometimes, Albert Wade was more than a friend. Him and the others who rode with Doc, they were my only family.

Suddenly, the bedroom door opened all the way, and Doc's enormous, tall frame loomed there in shadow.

"You got something to say, boy?"

I shut my eyes, tight, not wanting to see.

Chapter Eight

"Take a look at this, Gus."

Doc dropped a heavy glove on my shoulder.

"Nolan and Grimes took out of here with the horses. Kid Wade went with 'em," I said.

Eyes still closed.

"Sure, sure. I figured as much. But take a look at this."

I hesitated.

"What do you think of it?"

I steeled myself for whatever wonders of nature I might behold.

I opened my eyes.

And glory be—Doc Middleton was fully dressed.

But hells bells if he wasn't holding a gun barrel right under my nose just like he did the day I first met him.

I skedaddled back like a stray cat, keeping eyes on the nickel-plated barrel, asking him what the hell?

"Ain't it a hoot?" he said. "Been wantin' one of these for a long time."

The Colt single-action army pistol glowed with a blue-black finish in the dim lantern light spilling out from Trudy's room. Engraved whorls decorated the cylinder, and the butt was walnut. Doc held the gun at arm's length.

Pointed straight at my face.

Each one of the cartridge holes looked big and deep as a root cellar. It seemed like I could smell powder fill the room, could taste its rancid bitterness in the back of my throat. My eyes stung with imaginary smoke.

"Feel of it, August John."

It took a few seconds to realize he was offering me the chance to examine the gun. He wasn't going to shoot me.

When I took the weapon in hand, he crowed like a new papa and showed me a cardboard ammunition box. "Forty-five caliber."

The box was covered with a fancy script: *Twelve Revolver Ball Cartridges–Caliber .45–Frankford Arsenal, 1876.*

The pistol was heavy for its size, and it rested flat on my palm like a rock.

I was unsure what to do with it.

Polished to a fine shine with its intricate scrolls above the trigger, it looked to have never been fired.

I returned Doc's expectant expression. What to say?

"It's a fine piece."

"It's a goddamn treasure." He snatched the gun from my hand and shoved it into the waistband of his pants. "Mark my words, this little jewel will come in handy one day. Them bullets can pack a punch, let me tell you. It's the kind of thing a man might use to make a name for himself. They're calling this here hog's leg the *Peacemaker.* What a hoot."

Doc folded his arms in triumph, and Trudy joined him in the doorway, her lovely features radiant with calm satisfaction.

She had clothes on, too.

I felt foolish for imagining otherwise.

"Well, I better be on my way," said Doc. "Like the kid says, them others are already a mile down the trail ahead of me."

Over Trudy's shoulder, I could see inside her bedroom. The area was tidy and neatly arranged with a feather mattress on a log frame. A sturdy bedside table held up a coal-oil lamp, and a humpback trunk sat at the foot of the bed.

An oblong box sprawled open across the blankets.

It was the same kind of box Sonny Clausen had carried away in his wagon. I wondered if Clausen's box, like the one on Trudy's bed, was *full of guns*? Or maybe it was him bringing in the guns to start with?

Doc pulled my attention away from the bedroom with a husky tone. "I s'pose you want to ride along with me?"

"If you say so."

Doc replaced his hand on my shoulder and squeezed.

"Your comings and goings aren't my say-so. Never have been. Not since the day we met outside Julesburg."

I sort of shrugged, not sure where the conversation was going.

Doc cocked his head and stroked his fine mustache with his free thumb. "I admire you, Gus. Do you know it?"

"I reckon I always thought so."

Again, he squeezed my shoulder.

I wasn't sure what he meant, so I kept quiet.

"You're the kind of man I like being around. You're not like the others."

Squeeze.

"No, sir, you ain't like Windy or Boots or Albert."

It felt funny him saying Al's name in the same breath as the dead men. Did he know Boots and Windy were dead?

I wondered if maybe he wanted me to say something about them. Or if maybe he was trying to tell me something.

Doc gave my shoulder an extra pat. "I want you to stay here with Trudy. Watch out for her. Watch out for Pleasant Valley."

Surprise.

I caught a glimpse of Trudy's face flushing a mite pink before turning away to slide her bedroom door closed. I could only imagine how my own expression beamed like a beet.

Doc continued with his speechifying. "Every place needs

somebody to stand guard over it, to act as law."

It's how he thought of himself, a leader in the community, standing guard, acting as some kind of law. I believe it's why he wanted the Peacemaker so bad. In fact, he'd often rail on about the day when he would finally wear a star on his shirt and be a bona fide lawman—and, you know, later on in life, he was.

"Gus, it's your job to take care of this lady."

"I . . . uh . . . I ain't sure the two of us here together would be proper."

"Proper? Who taught you such a word?"

"It's just . . ."

"Don't you like girls, son?"

"It's not that."

"Don't you like Trudy?"

All of a sudden I felt all bashful like a five-year-old kid. " 'Course I like Trudy," I whispered.

"It's settled," Doc said and strode for the door. "Somebody's gotta be here to pull the calf, and you're elected for the job."

My head shot up so fast, I almost swallowed my tongue.

"Pull what calf?"

Doc gave me a military salute and carried his tall frame and its occupant Peacemaker out the front door into the rain.

I spun around on my bootheel.

"What's he talking about a calf?"

Trudy talked all at once, explaining in a flurry. "Doc took a look at the heifer while you were outside with the others. Her water's gonna break anytime. I'm sure it'll be okay. Not to worry. You don't have to stay if you don't want."

Glory be.

Here I was living like a husband and an animal husband both all at once.

And Lord have mercy, Trudy was selling guns from her bedroom.

When Trudy and I got outside to the barn, Doc was long gone after the others, and all I could see of Little Wound's horses was an acre of churned up mud turf and some busted fence rails.

Inside the barn, the rain was blowing in on the front stalls, and the heifer was soaking wet.

A uniform dusky brownish-gray, her good eye was clear and dark, the hair of her forehead course and curly. At some point during the morning, a glistening, bulbous water bag had slipped out of her vulva, and her stiff, shit-covered tail arced away from her back end.

"How long's her water been showing?"

"Since before breakfast," Trudy said. "Probably long enough to be trouble."

"It's maybe why Doc said what he did. Heifers generally take longer to calf than an experienced cow, maybe a few hours, but we might need to help her along. I need to get a closer look."

Without a thought, I jumped in with the critter to get a hackamore around her nose, but she rolled me onto my butt as she swung her iron-like skull at me like a sledgehammer.

She was a polled heifer, meaning her horns had been cut, and though she weighed a lot less than most of the old bossies I used to work growing up, she was young and anxious as any first-time mother. The contractions wracked her frame, leaving her confused, and she was literally blind on the pink-eye side. She bellowed, clomping forward and back against the rear wall of her pen.

"Whoa, Betty."

My hope was to get her tied to one of the barn's support pillars and then use the pen's squeeze gate to hold her.

"Who's Betty?" Trudy said with a nervous laugh, and from

my corner of the pen I told her it was my name for the cow. I just hadn't ever mouthed it aloud.

Trudy said, "How do you know I wasn't already calling her something else?"

" 'Cause you always just said, *the heifer* or *the cow.* If you've already got a name, I'll call her whatever you say."

"I like Betty."

"Betty it is."

I righted my hat and climbed to my feet in the corner of the pen while Betty bellowed out another loud complaint.

Coming at her blind side, I tried again to work the tightly braided hemp loop onto her. Tail held high like a buggy whip, she danced away from me, snorting and annoyed. "It's gonna be okay, Betty."

By now I'd had enough of a look-see at her rear end to think there might be trouble.

After a few more tries, I got Betty secured by the snout, wrapping the free end of my rope around an oak support pillar. Naturally, she pulled at the restraint, but she stayed upright and didn't go down in the ass-end, which was good.

A long, horizontal wood-planked gate was hinged to a second post support in the corner of the stall close to Betty's nose. The squeeze gate, now wide open and tied to the barn wall, could be swung around to hem a cow against the parallel wall of the stall. Held stationary in a chute no wider than her body, it would be impossible for Betty to move side to side and more difficult for her to kick.

"I'm gonna need some lard, plus a bucket of hot, soapy water," I said. "And the makings for a couple cigarettes if you've got 'em."

"Give me a few minutes," she said, hurrying outside but poking her head back into the barn to say, "Cigarettes?"

"Those are for me, not the cow."

"I'll do my best."

I crawled out of the pen and whistled "Dingleberry" while I waited, then pitched three forkfuls of dry hay from the rear pen into Betty's stall. The newborn would need a place to lie, and in the meantime the bedding would help dry up some of the damp dirt floor.

I'd stopped carrying my own tobacco about a year ago, because Albert was always bumming smokes off me, and I can't say I missed the habit. But standing alone in the shadows, breathing the haystack dust, I felt myself shake. A good long draw off a burning leaf would make things better for me and Betty both.

Thinking back to what Al had said about Trudy needing to have a good cow, I vowed to make sure of it.

As soon as she returned with a bucket of lard and a pail of water slick with lye soap, I rolled up my sleeves.

"Let's have the smoke," I said.

Trudy handed me a fat little canvas sack of tobacco and some rolling papers. After I had the curly smoldering, I climbed back into Betty's pen, lips pressed tight.

Trudy helped lift the bucket over the railings into the stall, then climbed across to join me.

"I'm going to need you to help with the squeeze gate," I said through a stream of smoke.

Betty's dirty behind faced our way, and my heart raced again as the young cow strained with exhaustion. Along with the dripping water sack and strands of goo hanging down, a jellied gray baby hoof and shiny flat nose peeked out from inside the cow.

I'd seen dozens of calves delivered in my life, most frontwards, a few backwards, one or two kitty-cornered like you wouldn't think possible. Only two of them died, and one was born dead, but a few had to be fixed along the way.

It was never a good sign when both front feet don't appear,

and Trudy knew it as well as I did. "I'll bet you this calf's got a leg bent up inside," she said.

I untied the swing gate and pulled it around, coaxing Betty into a smaller and smaller space.

When I got her shut up as tight as could be, she realized it and started kicking. It was all Trudy and I could do together to get the latch rope on the gate pulled tight across Betty's hocks and then tie it to the stall rail.

She shuffled around a bit, bawling, her sides puffing in and out like an accordion, and I soaped my right arm in the pail—all the while puffing smoke, burning the cigarette down to a nub.

"I believe you're right about the calf's leg," I said, making my arm good and slippery. "I'll need to shove the baby back up the canal by the nose, then reach in and try to straighten the bent leg so's he can slide out."

Betty's breathing was harder now, and her front legs trembled. There was just enough play in the hackamore rope to let her sink down onto her front knees, and her brisket rested on piles of hay. Each time she pushed, the baby calf's nose and toes extended past its dewclaw, then withdrew, the bent leg keeping it inside. If I didn't get a move on, the calf could suffocate in its mother's own slime-sack mucus.

At Betty's protruding side, Trudy leaned hard against the squeeze gate, her cheek touching the bristling cowhide, her chin taking splinters from the wood gate.

"You okay?" I said.

She nodded, but tears were coming down across her cheeks.

"What's wrong?"

She shook her head and flicked away the tears with her fingers. "Just save my calf, August John."

I think the whole size of the thing was dawning on her. Up until then, I guess I thought of Trudy as a rough and tumble homesteader type, more than familiar with the often crude and distasteful world of nature and its consequences.

After all, she wasn't exactly a candidate for the convent, running the station by herself, dealing in guns and ammunition. Hadn't she set up shop with a husband and gone through the pain of him leaving?

As it turns out, she was tougher than I ever might've imagined, but more tender, too, and a worrier. To face the thought of dead livestock, calf or cow, was a bigger deal back in those days than maybe it is now. Trudy had a soft heart, but, still, she was counting on both animals to fulfill her bigger picture of survival in Pleasant Valley.

I didn't think it was the right time to ask if running guns was more or less financially lucrative than cattle.

After greasing up my arm with lard, I put my fingers gently against the infant calf's nose, then slid over and cupped his foreleg, pushing, gently pushing the package back into the young cow. Her sides shuddered, and she pushed against me.

Once inside, I'd need to find the bent leg and draw it out straight into the pelvic canal—all by sense of touch. It had been a while since I pulled a calf, so I relaxed, closed my eyes, and breathed in smoke from the butt dangling at my lip.

On cue, Betty leaned hard into the gate, straining the tie rope, bearing down on my arm.

My fingers brushed the bent, bony knee. "Got it," I said, but if Trudy was relieved, she didn't show it. I let the cigarette fall from my lip to the stall floor, and Trudy stepped it out in the damp dirt and chaff.

Betty squeezed down, blocking all the blood from my tired arm. As a million hornets stung at my wrist and hand, my fingers felt like iron weights. I was up to my shoulder in cow, and damned but I couldn't find the baby calf's leg to grab it, couldn't move much at all, so I slipped out and leaned back against the stall rail, breathing heavy, dripping with blood.

As we watched, the baby's nose protruded out ever so much.

"Should I try?" Trudy said.

"Naw. If I ain't got the strength, you ain't got the strength."

"You're saying you ain't got the strength?"

"I didn't mean it like so."

"You going back in?"

"Of course, I am." I knelt down to the bucket of water and slopped up my arm. "Make me another smoke, will you?"

Next time went better. After only a few minutes, I was able to get a firm grip on the calf's leg and pull it out straight. Betty got pretty feisty and tried to give Trudy a kick to the shin, but the gate blocked her cement hoof.

I could feel the calf coming now, moving out like it was supposed to, and Betty sunk down to lay flat on her belly. Heaving and bawling, she slammed the gate again, this time cracking it dead center, the extra leeway allowing her to lay over.

Trudy backed off and moved the bucket out of the way, and I joined her as the new little life slid onto the floor of the stall, covered in a glittering pink and blood-covered membrane.

Fast as a June bug, I crouched down, had my fingers all over the calf's face, clearing the mucus from its nose and mouth, swiping at its tongue and eyes. The little devil coughed and gagged, tried to raise its head and kick its feet all at the same time.

"You did it, Gus," Trudy said.

"We did it. You've got a fine little bull there, Trudy."

"I've got some towels."

Before long the two of us had the newborn rubbed down and ready to stand on a shaky quartet of legs, his tan hair in disarray, his puzzled expression adding to the comedy. Trudy left the pen, and I yanked the squeeze gate free, then untied the hackamore.

Betty went straight to her offspring and nosed him into a standing position.

On shaky legs, the calf bleated out a complaint and pitched over forward onto his chin, causing his rump to roll in sideways.

"Human beings take eight months to walk, and cows take eight minutes. Doesn't seem fair somehow."

"Fair enough," I said. "A few years from now, this fellow will be roasted and on somebody's supper plate."

"Betty's getting nervous with such talk. Let's leave these two alone for a while."

We both knew the young bossy couldn't understand a word of English, but after coming close to losing the little bull, it was fun to josh about it. I jumped over the edge of the stall and sent a few chickens running for cover.

"Them chickens heard you talking about supper."

"I hadn't thought much about dinner or supper, either one, after the gorgeous breakfast you served us."

"I'm humbled by the compliment, sir."

"Birthin' calves is hard work. How about a gorgeous dinner?"

The sky outside was still dark and gloomy, but Trudy's smile made up for the lack of sun. "We might be back to beans and hardtack."

She seemed ten times more chipper with the others gone, and, realizing how we were alone in the sheltering barn, my tongue swelled to twice its size, and I was shy to say more.

She didn't make things easy.

"About all these men coming and going from my bedroom," she began, and I nearly jumped out of my skin.

"I'm sure it's . . . all, uh . . . proper," I said.

"There it is again. In all my days, I've never heard a Pony Boy use the word proper."

"I'm trying to . . . increase my vocabulary."

She kept her chin down but looked up at me from beneath

long, tender lashes. "Oh, what are some other new words you know?"

Sweetheart.

Darling.

She was fishing around for some mush, but I was skittish and hungry, and, after all, it wasn't quite noontime yet.

"I know some words, but I ain't used to saying them," Trudy said. She walked close to me and looked up into my face. I could feel her breath on my chin and pick out every strand of damp hay mixed into her hair. We both smelled more like Betty than ourselves.

"Uh . . . um, what words are those?"

She pushed her breasts against my chest and wrapped her arms around me.

"Thank you," she said. "For Betty . . . for understanding about Doc. For being kind to Albert."

When she tilted her chin up a second time, I kissed her on the mouth.

"He really is my cousin," she said.

I kissed her again.

We stayed there in the barn for a long time.

Chapter Nine

My mouth got quite the workout during the next few days.

More smoochin' than I'd done for a while, but more talking, too. And boy, did I eat.

After pulling the calf, Trudy and I spent most of the following morning with a teamster named Timmons unloading a wagon of goods to the station shelves. Fifty-some dollars' worth of everything from cornmeal to canned applesauce. No way either one of us was going to go hungry.

Timmons threw in a big ox bone for Moses McGee and some extra salt just for Betty. He said dosing her regular diet of cracked corn and hay would help her milk, and heaven help me if it didn't.

The newborn calf—we called him Buddy—ate a good supper at the end of his first official day of life, but I had to help him get started.

Inside the house, Trudy and me did okay. Trudy cooked a pair of venison steaks Timmons brought, fried a mess of potatoes with onions, and topped it off with cornbread, butter, and sorghum.

Pretty soon, I found out Trudy was serious about her Bible reading, so I left her to it around nine o'clock.

It was still early with summer coming on and it being light outside. I kicked around my bedroll in the barn, full of stomach but restless of spirit. Moses paced around with me, and every now and then I sat for several minutes and just scratched his ears while he cooled his tongue.

Boots and Windy were weighing more heavy than ever on my soul. I couldn't help but figure somehow our run to Pine Ridge was partly to blame, but I couldn't put a finger on who would string 'em up in such a way.

Little Wound was always having trouble keeping his young men from the vengeance trail, and I thought about those two with their new rifles.

The more I beat my brains over it, the more scared I got.

Now Kid Wade was out there with Doc and Curley Grimes, and shrinking down next to my bedroll I came to realize I didn't trust a darned one of them with Al's well-being.

The sun had disappeared behind the abandoned corrals, and the first stars blinked into life when Trudy crept in and liked to scare the liver out of me and Moses.

But the hound didn't bark.

"Are you asleep, Gus?"

My heart stopped, then started again with a jolt, and I popped up from my bedroll on a scabby elbow wishing I had Kid Wade's gun. I needed to buy one of Trudy's spares.

"It's just me," Trudy said.

"Dammit, you knocked the wind outta me."

"I didn't mean to wake you up."

"Oh, I wasn't sleeping. Just surprised me."

Moses did a little jig and Trudy patted his back, calming him down.

"It's dark out here," she said.

"I like the dark."

"Want to talk?"

"Do you want to talk?"

She walked into the open stall, stepping over my bedroll.

"I don't like the dark."

"Ain't no reason to be afraid of anything."

"Booses, waspers, Dáxte-Wáu."

"Who's Dáxte-Wáu ?"

"The Santee deer-woman."

"Wait, wait, hold up. What's a booses?" I'd heard all the Indian legends about deer-ladies and bear-men, and giant sea-snakes in the Niobrara, poking their heads out of the water. But I'd never heard of the first thing she said.

"Booses are the wandering spirits of dead children. They play pranks on you in the dark."

"I've never heard of booses before. You ever see any?"

"They roam these hills like lightning bugs, quick, crafty."

"You're giving me goose pimples. I'm not kidding."

"I've seen plenty of booses. Especially in the winter."

"Thank goodness it's on to May."

"I finished reading my Bible."

"What'd you learn about tonight?"

She laughed and spread her dress out around her as she sat down on the floor, her back against the outer barn wall. "Would you believe, I don't rightly recall?"

To me, the Good Book is dry as fall gamma grass, so I wasn't surprised.

"Must've been pretty exciting," I said.

"Too many begats to keep track of."

"I always got stuck in the begats."

"I don't take you for a Bible reader."

"I didn't take you for selling guns to people."

It just slipped out, and when Trudy didn't say anything, I followed up quick. "I mean, it just sorta surprised me when I saw you selling guns to Doc. And Clausen—hoo boy! How'd you end up being a gun runner?"

"It's not something a person plans on doing. At least I didn't. It just sort of happened to me. Do you know what I mean?"

"I never did do anything I planned on," I said. "Albert and

me, we avoid planning. Gets in the way of our fun."

The two of us took turns scratching Moses under the chin.

Before long, the old boy was sprawled out between us, snoring.

"Doc doesn't buy a whole lot of guns," Trudy said. "Just now and again he picks up something he's interested in—like the pepper gun. There's a few others I sell carbines to."

"Indians?"

"I don't sell to Indians. Some folks do."

I let it lie, wondering how a gal like Trudy got hooked into such a scheme. I still didn't know where the guns came from.

But after a while she still hadn't said anything more.

She was so pretty sitting there as moonlight shined through the barnwood gaps to draw vertical silver lines on her face.

I figured I had spoiled our talk, so I let my fingers sneak over to touch her hand.

She didn't pull away. Relieved, I sat up and scootched over so I was right beside her, and I could feel the warmth of her arm beside mine.

She kissed my forehead, and we cuddled for a spell, and out of the blue she said, "Let's play a game."

I thought she meant cards. I'm not much for cards, having never quite got the hang of so many different rules for so many different hands.

I told her so, but she said, *no,* not a card game.

"Let's play, *I've got a secret.*"

On top of everything else, I didn't think it was a good idea because I had plenty of secrets needing to stay secret.

"I'd be willing to take a crack at the cards," I said. "I hear Sheephead's a fine game."

"My secret is something you've already wondered about."

"If you'd rather not . . ."

"I want to," she said. "I've been alone out here for more than a year, and I'm tired of randy old men and cranky sodbusters. You're the first man to show a caring attitude toward me for nothing in return."

Which wasn't exactly true. I'd got plenty in return, and I had the full stomach to prove it. But I let it go.

"What about the wives of all these visitors?" I said.

"Their wives don't often come with 'em."

I remembered the dirty thoughts I'd had about Trudy soon after I saw her with Clausen, and I felt ashamed. I figured she wasn't a clear-water spring, not at her age—she was a good bit older than me, surely pushing thirty.

But so far her Bible reading came between the two of us well enough, and I wasn't about to push her anyway. What Albert had told Squeaky was more truth than kidding. I hadn't been around so many females unless you count bovines, mares, and a mess of mud hens.

"Okay, a game then," I said. "You've got a secret. What's my part supposed to be?"

"You've got three guesses. If you don't get it, you've got to tell a secret on yourself."

"What if I don't have anything to tell?"

Boots and Windy's eyes bulged out at me from the darkness.

"Everybody has a secret to tell," Trudy said.

You can always tell a horse thief by the way he swings a rope.

One minute the barn was warm with the coming of summer, and I had my arms full of a healthy young lass.

The next minute winter set in.

Betty bawled and the calf mewled, and I said, "Maybe I ought to check on them two."

"They're fine," Trudy said. "Are you going to play the secret game?"

I swallowed hard. "I guess so."

"My secret is about Albert."

"About how you're related to him?"

"Just so." She leaned forward expectantly.

"Well . . . Albert's dad gifted you the pump, so I know about him and you."

The answer caught her off guard, and she sat back with a huff, kicking her bare feet in the hay.

I couldn't figure her reaction.

"I was just starting my guess, but I'm right so far, aren't I? Aren't I? Trudy?"

When she turned her face away, her expression melted into the shadows of the barn, and all I could see was her jawline and ear lined up in the moon. But she sure was upset.

"Hey . . . hey, gal."

She kicked the hay again, and this time gave me a backhanded swat.

I wondered how she could be so much older than me but act so much younger at the same time.

"Go to hell," she said.

"Let's don't be childish," I said, which was absolutely the wrong thing to say.

She turned on me like a bobcat.

"Childish? I'll tell you what's childish, *August John.* Childish is you and Albert Wade out here laughing and making fun of me while I'm in there cleaning slobber off your supper plates and washing your clothes."

"Wait, what? Did you wash Albert's clothes? Because, you didn't wash *my* clothes."

"You never asked."

"Well, there's a fine howdy-do. I've been wearing this same shirt and pants for about two weeks."

"How long you've worn your clothes is no secret. I can smell you coming before you open the door."

"My secret? I didn't know we were still playing."

"He told you, didn't he? Albert told you about his stepfather."

"He told me about the pump—"

"So what if I was his girlfriend? So what if I let him stay with me? I got a nice, shiny new pump out of it, didn't I? I got Betty, and now I've got a calf."

"Whoa, now, hold up a sec—"

"Don't give me some bunch of morals, August John. Don't you dare preach at me. I may have lost my virtue to the sonuvabitch, but I still have my dignity. I get by on my own, and I don't need some pony boy telling me how to live."

I gently cupped my hand over her mouth and took stinging rebuke for it.

Trudy pushed away my hand and slapped my face.

"Nobody's preaching," I said. "You don't know what I was gonna say."

"I've got a good idea."

We sat staring into each other's moonshine eyes, and I understood then what she was saying.

The drummer Albert had mentioned, the one who brought Trudy to Pleasant Valley, but then abandoned her.

It was his stepfather.

John Wade, born of Scotch immigrants in NewYork, moved to Iowa with his parents, landing in Niobrara City and then Springfield, Bon Homme County, in Dakota territory before filing on a couple homesteads in the area. Around the time all of this was happening, Wade had uprooted himself and his family again, living close to Big Sandy Creek. Everybody I knew thought John was Al's father because they shared the same last name, but Kid Wade called him a drunken "step-rooster." Sometimes he claimed to hardly know him.

Like me, Al left home early.

We'd been on our own together for a long time.

Apparently, John Wade had had a dalliance with Trudy.

I chose my words carefully. "It doesn't matter what Albert is to you," I said. "Or the old man, either. Let's put on some coffee, and you teach me a game of cards, huh?"

Trudy sobbed freely now, her shoulders quaking under her cotton dress. When she looked up again, she seemed as helpless as Betty's calf. "I only wanted to tell you Albert truly is my cousin. That was my secret. He's related to me on his mother's side, a couple times removed. I wanted you to know we weren't neither one of us lying to you, Gus."

She leaned toward me, and I took her in my arms.

"I wasn't planning to tell you the other thing," she said.

"I didn't mean to hurt you." I kissed her hair. "I would never hurt you."

"It wasn't so long ago. But it seems like forever John has been gone, out to Big Sandy with his wife and kids. Albert's got sisters, you know."

"I know. I know his family."

"Then you know John."

"Not real well."

"Nobody knows him well. Least of all, me."

"Shhh," I said. "Let's not talk about him."

"I haven't seen him since he brought Betty over as a calf. Just dumped her on my step. I guess he still felt he owed me something. Probably he stole her from somebody and wanted to get rid of the evidence."

"After Al told me about where you got your new pump, I had thought, sort of offhand, maybe it was Al's stepfather who supplied your . . . uh, bedroom inventory? Is he your source for guns?"

She clucked her tongue. "I get the guns from Sonny Clausen. The day you and Albert showed up, I was just taking in a shipment."

The oblong box in Clausen's wagon had been *empty*. Well,

surprise, surprise.

"Where's Clausen get the guns to start with?"

"There's no way to know. I don't ask, and you shouldn't either."

"You buy them direct from him, or pay him a percentage?"

"Sixty percent," she said.

"Sounds like the dirty end of the pitchfork."

"He says he's the one taking all the risks." After a few seconds, she added, "I said before, I don't sell to Indians. I leave it for Sonny."

"He's supplying them carbines?"

"Ponca and Santee Sioux. Yes, he sells them rifles."

"Might not be such a good idea."

Her tone was halfway defiant. "Indian money spends as good as any."

I squeezed her tight and rocked her in my arms. All our scuffling around had Moses up and about, which upset Betty.

I decided it was better to be outside under the stars.

Together we walked across the range toward the corrals, and her voice was stronger the farther away from the barn we got. Like the fresh night air cleared her head.

She said, "You don't have to tell me your secret if you don't want to."

"Wouldn't hardly be fair, would it?"

"I was being fresh. I'm sorry."

"No," I said. "No . . . you shared something with me, and now I've got an obligation."

I considered telling her about my ma, the old bat I'd left back behind Old Baldy, and the squalor of the house she ran with a willow switch.

In a way, Trudy had divulged something about her family life; I wanted to do likewise.

But the same untold story kept coming to mind, the same

grisly discovery waiting out there in the cottonwood grove under a pile of brush.

If I didn't tell somebody about Boots and Windy, I'd bust.

"Me and Albert vowed never to tell anybody about it, but I need you to come with me."

Booses and waspers and Indian deer-ladies be damned.

I held Trudy's hand tight and led her straight to the ghastly death scene.

And, of course, the bodies were gone.

Chapter Ten

We passed the next several weeks like an old married couple during the day and a couple of church mice at night. Trudy holed up with her Bible and I kept watch out in the barn.

I fixed up the place where it was needed, feeding and watering Betty and the horses. Trudy cooked and did up my laundry, going so far as to replace my socks with a fine new cotton store-bought pair, and she fixed up a new buckskin shirt for me, not unlike the one Albert wore.

The calf was growing but had trouble sucking because of Betty's swollen tits, and I had to help him get ahold of her three or four times each day.

It was Dill Schiller who showed up one warm afternoon out of the blue with a wagon full of tin, a sack of homemade donuts, and Doc Middleton's wedding invite.

When I heard his horse coming in, I stepped outside the station house to greet him. "How do, Dill?"

He had sugar frosting all over his face. "Long time, Gus. How ya been?"

I told him I'd been fine as cock robin. "What's all this?" I said, meaning the pile of tin in the buckboard bed. I saw dozens of sorry bent-up cups and plates, but some cheerful white enamelware pots.

"It's a living is what it is. How much you want to buy?"

"I don't know if we're buying."

"We?" Dill indicated the whole of Pleasant Valley with his

chin. "You part of Trudy's hacienda now, Gus? You two make it all official, did you?"

I didn't want to agree with him, but it would do little good to say otherwise. Dill's wagging tongue was as bad as Sonny Clausen's. The kid would have us married with twins, and everybody in the Niobrara valley would know about it before the end of the weekend.

"Doc Middleton asked me to stay with her. Watch out for undesirables." I hoped by mentioning Doc's name, Dill would think twice about running off at the mouth. Just to be sure, I patted the wheel gun on my belt.

Dill wasn't overly impressed. "We're carrying a six-shooter, now, are we?"

"I don't know about you, but I am. Like I said. Been watching out for things."

Dill wasn't sure how to take my comments, which didn't hurt a thing. I liked keeping him on his toes. I guess I considered him an old pal—but the truth was, I hadn't laid eyes on him since the day he cut out, back when Otto Randolph said Doc might be killed.

"What've you been up to, Dill? Do any riding with Albert?"

"Not for a while. He's over at Doc's—getting in pretty thick with Curley Grimes."

"You ridin' with Doc?"

"Pickin' up a horse or two of my own now and then. I've got a nice pair of Red Duns you ever want to see 'em."

My stomach didn't like the sound of Dill working by himself or Albert and Curley Grimes being so chummy, so I changed the subject.

"Trudy's inside with some coffee. I'm sure she'd welcome them doughnuts."

Dill shoved the bag under my nose. "He'p yourself."

"Don't mind if I do."

Dill clambered down from the wagon, and I led his two horses over to the edge of the stream behind the house. We'd had a nice shower the night before, and there was a fresh drink for the pair of broomtails.

More than water oughtn't be necessary, I thought.

It was still early in the afternoon, and Dill needed to get about his business—whatever it was—and move on. Like I said, I didn't trust him as much as I once might've.

At the time I didn't realize how I'd set my feather not just for Trudy, but for all of Pleasant Valley. Or maybe it was the other way around: maybe the lonesome canyon saw the steward it needed. Maybe it wrapped its stickery tendrils and gnarled mulberry and elm roots around my ambitions, roping me into a lifetime love affair, bittersweet but eternal.

I watched the horses slurp up enough to part the Red Sea, and I breathed untainted high-plains air.

Presently, Trudy and Dill came back outside, her wiping her hands on a towel, him carrying a square of paper.

I'll never forget the day, May 27, 1879, because I saw the date scrawled across the envelope Dill handed me.

"Did you get what you needed?" I asked. "We're low on some items."

Trudy had yet to receive any new carbines from Clausen, and I couldn't help but wonder if my living there had something to do with it. Or maybe the old sumbuck's source was drying up. I'd been thinking more and more about how it wasn't a good life for Trudy. All these strangers coming around at odd hours.

Trudy held up the sack of doughnuts, the brown paper dark and grease stained at the bottom. Dill's reply was kinda sheepish, and now I saw why maybe he thought Trudy and I had tied the knot. Marriage was on his mind.

"Really, I just drove over to deliver this."

Under the date on the envelope, somebody had printed my

name in careful block letters. The back flap was stuck shut with a piece of sealing wax. If we lived in some fancy, faraway land, it would be impressed by a king's signet ring or something.

Here on the Running Water, somebody had mashed it with a calloused thumb.

I tore open the end and took out a crooked cut slip of paper.

I'm marrying Pood Richardson. Would like you to be there. Bring Trudy.

Which is all it said. No greeting. No signature.

"Doc told you to give this to me?"

"Ah-yuh," Dill said.

"Where and when?"

"Yesterday, at Morris's."

"No, I meant, where and when is the wedding?"

Dill stuck out an elbow to scratch the back of his neck. "I reckon it's tomorrow sometime at Richardson's place on the north side of the Running Water. Ol' Henry ain't keen on the whole thing. Guess Doc asked for Pood's hand in matrimony, and the old man chewed him raw."

"But he's hosting the wedding anyway?"

"Henry ain't planning to be there. Ain't a whole lot he can do about it anyway." Dill cleared his throat. "We're all gonna be at the Jake Haptonstall house. It's where Pood and Ted and their mom's been staying. You know where it is?"

I held the invitation up to the wind. Pood's proper name was Mary, and folks said she was an odd duck who never took her clothes off, not to sleep, not to bathe . . . never. Her cousin, Ted, was a bit younger than me.

"This is official, right? They're gonna have a preacher and everything?"

"They got old Skinner to do it. He's been living in a tent around the south side of the river with his wife, so I guess Doc will put him to good use."

There didn't seem to be much more to say, so Dill crawled into his wagon and made ready to shove off.

Before he left, he tipped back his straw hat.

"You ain't seen Boots Harper or Windy Barnes have you?"

"No, I ain't seen 'em. Why?"

"They haven't been around much. It's not like Windy to be so lost."

"Maybe they'll show up for the wedding."

"Yeah," Dill said, "Maybe they will at that."

I didn't have the heart to tell him why they wouldn't.

Trudy and me got up early the next morning to ride down to the wedding, but by the time we got Betty and Buddy situated and Moses McGee set up inside the station with food and water to act as guard, we didn't roll around to Richardson's spread until midafternoon.

The homeplace wasn't as highfalutin as it should've been considering how many cows Henry ran on all his fat pastureland.

Henry's wife, Anne, lived with Pood and her nephew, Ted Roberts, in the Haptonstall house, an ancient four-walled hornet's nest hung together with flour paste and fishing line. Swear to heaven, they had a roll of string tying one of the shutters in place.

Gossip had Henry building a new luxury residence for them up north sometime before winter.

If they ever did, by God, I never saw it.

But they weren't stuck up on themselves like a lot of rich people.

Half a dozen wagons greeted us when we pulled in the lane, and I counted eight horses tied up at the hitch in front of the house. There weren't much of a shelterbelt around the place—a few elm and boxelder. Cottonwoods. Not half as much shade as over at Heavy Frahm's place but more than we had at Pleasant Valley, where the station sat out in the full daylight.

I worried about all the horses standing around with no shade, but Trudy said somebody, maybe one of the little kids, would keep 'em watered.

There was a tenfold flock of kids—all of them running up and down the hill between the ramshackle house and a wide-open pole pavilion.

Anyway, the sour old house needed a good whitewashing, but Anne had some coneflowers plunked down around the split front boardwalk, so I guess it was a start.

"Aren't the flowers pretty?" Trudy said.

I thought they were real purty, purple petals arranged around iron red.

"They're blooming plenty early this year."

"Six weeks of rain to the old timers' thinking."

"It wouldn't dare rain on Doc's wedding day."

If it did, the guests would blow the clouds from the sky, filling the air with enough lead to sink a paddleboat. I remember thinking it because almost all the men I saw carried firearms.

Most of them I knew, and some were just passing familiar. Some I didn't recognize, and some I never could figure out why they were there.

The air from the pole barn was full of the warm smell of roast pig where they had a good size hunk of pork cooking on a spit.

Trudy and I climbed down from the wagon, me in my best set of black Sunday britches, suit coat, and a wide-brimmed hat. Trudy wore a long, green dress which must have cost old John Wade a lot, because green was an expensive color to get. It was real chipper with a lot of lace at the bottom and around the neck. She had her hair pulled behind her neck in a loose bun.

Trudy was beautiful, and I felt like a lucky man to be carrying her to the party.

The first feller spoke to us was none other than old Sonny Clausen.

"Lookee who's here," he said.

I didn't feel like getting into one of Clausen's long-winded stories, so I sorta hung back like I was messing with one of the horses and told Trudy to go on and enjoy herself.

"If I see him, I'll send Doc over," she said, but she never did.

"You not talking today, August John?"

"Got a twist in the traces," I said, still standing beside the horse.

A small gent, wrinkled and bald, drank with Clausen. Standing together beside the hitch, sipping from tin cups, they might've been brothers except Clausen had a thick gut and wild, wiry hair. The lizard-skinned man was clean shaven and bald with sneaky eyes and looked like a stiff wind would turn him over sideways. He was half my size, but two days older than dust.

Clausen held up his cup.

"You get'cher rig fixed, come on over and get a snort."

"What'cha got?"

"Rum, if you can believe it."

"Never had any rum."

The little man said, "It's too damn sweet," and his voice was like the cheep of a songbird. I could've knocked him over with a flick of my hat. "I gots to get some of the pork. Hate to drink on an empty stomach."

"You're carrying a new pistolero there, Gus."

Clausen's words were starting to slur, but there was nothing wrong with his eyes.

With Boots and Windy's remains gone missing, I bartered away half my war bag to Trudy for the gun on my hip.

"It's a new double-action revolver," I said.

Clausen made his words boom. “Thunder.” He was the kind who always liked to put on a show.

“Yeah, it’s a .41.”

“Kid Wade carries the Lightning.” He said it like I wouldn’t know.

“Yes, he does.”

“ ’Spect he’ll be jealous of you.”

“Not Albert. You know him and me are chums.”

The lizard man’s laugh was whisper smooth, like a salt shaker. “Chums is the worst kind of jealous.”

For a second, I almost felt ashamed.

I never gave Albert a thought until now. It was true he might be jealous.

“He won’t care,” I said.

“Heard tell Doc bought a Colt .45 off your gal friend. Maybe he’ll buy another one today.”

“It’s between Trudy and Doc.”

“Leave it to James Riley Middleton to have business with another gal on the day of his nip-tuals.”

“Nuptials,” the lizard man said. “And don’t forget, today his name is Jim Sheppard of Paddock.” Doc was always using false names and aliases.

“Just today?” I said.

“It’s what’s on the marriage license.”

“First time I met him, he was called Jim Cherry.”

Lizard man got a kick out of the name.

“Speak of the devil, and he shall appear,” Clausen said.

I turned away from them expecting to see Doc, but instead here was Albert, halfways gussied up, like I hadn’t seen him except once at church, but not quite, because his white shirt was untucked, and his string tie stretched loose.

He carried his coat over his shoulder with a crooked finger. The opposite finger was looped through the stretched-out handle of a tin mug abundant with suds.

"Lookee who needs a beer."

"Howdy, Al."

"Where you been keeping yourself, Gus? Goddamn, it's good to see you."

He pushed the beer at me, sloshing a third of it onto my coat.

"Drink up."

I obliged him, and the warm, grainy flavor was thicker than expected, dragging my tongue toward the back of my throat. Like swallowing spoiled oatmeal.

Al slapped my shoulder. "You better come with me, boy. We got a lot of catching up to do."

"It's good to see you, Al."

"Good to see me," he said. "You might not think so after what I got to say. There's news, boy. And it's trouble."

I took another small sip of beer, moving my face from Albert to Clausen and his friend, then back. "I ain't heard of any trouble."

"You been domesticated, son. Why, it's the biggest thing to happen on the Running Water."

Clausen said, "He's talkin' about them Indians what shot a couple ranchers in the Sandhills."

"I guess I ain't heard."

"You go down and eat some pig, and keep your ears open," the little man said. "I was gonna go down there and eat. Sure do hate to drink on an empty stomach."

"Everybody's going crazy," Al said. "Old Little Wound has got a price on your head, pony boy. He ain't one to mess around with. You ask around, you'll hear about it. He was over there at Massacre Canyon warring with the Pawnee in '73. Hell of a fight it was."

I wasn't sure how to take what Al said. He was always kidding around, but this kind of talk shook me a little, and I gulped down too much beer. My stomach churned as Al flopped an arm around my shoulder and steered me away toward the crowd at the pavilion.

"Now look here, I'm without a drink," Al said.

His words were starting to slur worse than Clausen's.

"Lookit this turnout. What a grand day."

"What's this about a price on my head?"

"Aw, I shouldn't have skeered ya, Gus. It's just a couple braves got into the loco weed."

"But the men they killed?"

"Couple old ranchers keeping some Indian ponies the Sioux thought they shouldn't maybe be keeping."

"It is about stolen horses then?"

"Don't worry about it."

"Killed!" I said.

"Hey, we're going on a run tomorrow. Figure on being gone a week or more. I want you to come along."

"How can you go? With these Indians . . . ?"

"Some of the boys are out today. You might notice Count Shevaloff ain't here. Limber Dick ain't here." He rattled off four more names.

"Where are they?"

"Making a run at Spotted Tail's horses."

Now I understood. The others were gone without him, and it was working on Albert's patience. He didn't want to be shown up.

"So you're heading out tomorrow."

"Maybe take a run for some ponies over to the old Ponca agency." He paused, putting his thoughts together. "You might think I'm worried about the Indians shooting us, but I ain't worried about it at all. Like I say, everybody's a little crazy today. I think they're making hay where there's nothing but dirt." He chewed his lip and finally said, "It's some big damn news for normal people though."

Al saw a clump of men gathered a ways down the hill and stopped walking so fast, I bumped into him, dropping the stein into the dirt.

I was surprised how little was left inside to spill.

We stood still and looked at the fallen container like earth and sky had betrayed us.

Finally, Al regained some focus, slapped my back. "We'll get you another one of those."

Then he raised an arm to wave at the men he'd stopped to watch. "There's old Preacher Skinner. He's the one Doc got who's going to perform the ceremony."

I looked in the direction he pointed and saw more than one person I knew.

"There's Otto Randolph."

Randolph raised a hand in our direction. I waved, but Al did not.

"Tomorrow, I want you to come along with," Al said again. "We leave in the morning."

"Who's gonna take Trudy back home?"

"She'll manage."

"She shouldn't have to manage. Doc has me watching out for her."

"You always do what Doc says? Now you're talking like Dill Schiller. Doesn't sound like August John who dogged Jim Cherry out of his gun back in Julesburg." Albert cocked his head. "Anyway, Dill's going. Maybe George Holt."

Al turned away. "There's old Dill now over there with Black George."

"Dill and Black George?"

"Why not?"

"George can't ride worth a durn. You're crippled before you

get started."

"Which is why I need you, boy." He grinned. "Lookee over there. It's Jack Nolan talking to Doc."

Al's pointing out everybody was making me feel more at home.

The truth was, I was tempted by his invitation. I was just as jealous of Dill and Black George as Al was jealous of the other Pony Boys.

"You were right when you said everybody was here."

"Shoot, yes." Al smacked his lips. "I sure am thirsty."

If Al had noticed my gun, he didn't say anything. For his part, it appeared he carried his pistol in the pocket of his trousers, but his jacket covered up the imprint.

I thought about the wagon and horses again and glanced over my shoulder. Clausen and his pal were still jawboning away, and, from where we stood, the horses seemed perfectly comfortable.

"By the way," I said, "who was the little fellow we were talking to? The one who was drinking rum with Clausen?"

"You surely know who he was," Al said. But I told him I didn't.

Al pushed me back with surprise. "You don't know Heavy Frahm when you see him?"

"*That* was Heavy Frahm?"

I swear my jaw must've hung down a mile. I couldn't believe it.

I had never met the man, but I'd always assumed he was a giant.

"From the cathouse—*Heavy Frahm*?"

"Well, hell yes." Like I was dumb as ditch water.

"I mean . . . he . . . that little runt . . ." My stomach felt better then, and I started laughing.

"Yep. He's a runt, all right."

"I just never . . ." I couldn't stop laughing.

Al joined in, slapping me on the back. I can't remember ever laughing harder.

"I'll be go to the devil," I said.

"Not yet," Al said, pushing a lit cigarette into my mouth. "Not yet, but we're working on it."

Chapter Eleven

The beer left me empty headed but more cheerful than I'd been for a month of Sundays, and Al led me past the pole building with its clusters of men in various states of celebratory conversation. Doc's wedding had called out everybody who was anybody on the Niobrara.

I didn't tell Al I'd go with him in the morning on a pony run. But I didn't tell him I wouldn't. A week was a long time to leave Trudy by herself.

Turned out to be a lot longer.

Some folks say Doc's wedding was a somber affair, and maybe the ceremony was, and maybe not, but me and Al surely had some fun beforehand. There was a lot of cutting up and joking, and it was one of the last great wingdings we had before the awful trick they played on me.

I wasn't looking for it, and because of it, I hurt Trudy pretty bad. It's what you get when you're young and stupid and cocksure of yourself.

Al and me stopped a couple times in the hot sun to chat with the wedding guests. First with some rawboned old cowboys we knew from up north of the Keya Paha, and we got the mad Indian story again, about the ranchers being shot. One of the cowboys said he didn't blame the natives for being disagreeable.

What if those ranchers had been killed with Sonny Clausen's guns? Or Trudy's?

Then we talked to this silly sumbuck who claimed to be Jesse

James, the train robber from Missouri who hid out near us on the Running Water a few years before. Albert claimed he met the outlaw face to face, but I didn't believe him. Anyway, Al said, "I met Jesse face to face and his brother Frank, and you ain't neither one of them," and the old boy admitted he was just a Jesse James actor, and I said, "Dammit, ain't it the dumbest thing you ever heard?"

Why would anybody want to pass themselves off as somebody other than themselves?

Then Albert said maybe somebody would want to be a Kid Wade actor someday. When he was dead, his name would live on in books and legends. He was so full of himself.

He wanted to be remembered, especially by the girls.

Anyway, Jesse James was in Mississippi by then.

The truth is there were five men for every girl at Richardson's place, and, looking back on it now, every single fellow kept a gun on his belt or inside his pants. Which was uncommon for us in those days, no matter what anybody says. I didn't pay attention at the time, but it was because of those Indians running around.

There were a lot of kids tearing it up, because there's always kids horsing around at a wedding, giggling and making mad plans and cutting in front of a person.

Trudy was standing with a bunch of gals behind the barn.

One of the girls was smoking a cigarette. She had loud red hair and a pair of watermelons on her chest, and I thought it was Pood Richardson, Doc's bride. She sure looked like a handful.

By this time, Al and I had wandered farther down the hill, away from the hasty-cut lawn to a stickery patch where the Russian thistles were waist high and ropey. A bashful shed hid in the tall grass there, flat roofed like a chicken coop. I figured it was for keeping firewood or maybe storing shovels and rakes and so on. A loud splash came from the back, and we rounded the corner to find Dill and Ted Roberts fixing drinks under the direction of Curley Grimes.

The three of them stood around a five-gallon copper tub, the kind with wood handles attached to each side. Dill was pouring amber liquid from a brown bottle into a frothing sea.

The tub was near half full, the brew a sickly pink color. Laughing Al couldn't contain himself. He was still half tickled about me not knowing Heavy Frahm.

"What kind of sardine soup are you boys mixing?"

"Special recipe called Ol' Bowlegs," said Curley. Given the circumstances, it should've been a joke, and I guess Curley meant it to be, but his rumbling delivery made it sound like a warning.

Al said Curley never could sound jovial on account of the squaw's injury to his neck. But to me the scar didn't come anywhere near the damn sourpuss's vocal cords.

But that's me. I didn't like Curley.

Dill popped the cork on a ceramic jug, holding it up for Curley's approval and got a curt nod before upending it.

"Ol' Bowlegs'll turn your knees inside out."

"What's in the mix so far?"

Dill spilled the contents of the jug into the potion.

"Some of this, some of the other. Corn whiskey, rye, a stein of beer."

"How come it's pink?"

Ted said, "Got some mulberry wine in there."

He was a scrawny bird with spectacles and a bow tie. Most of the suits wore string ties—or whip ties they sometimes called 'em—with a polished stone clasp. Ted was a bit younger than me, afraid to say *boo,* and usually the others pushed him around too much. I could tell everybody was being friendly since it was his cousin tying the knot.

The strong odor coming off the jug curled my nose hair. "You're pouring the corn whiskey now?"

Albert dropped his fingers into the tub and flipped them back at me, splashing.

"Yes, ma'am, it's corn whiskey. Are we offending your delicate palate?"

It was the second funniest thing I'd heard all day, and everybody else thought so, too, since we all started to laugh.

Even Curley chuckled.

Dill dropped the jug and picked up a tin cup from the ground. After two big, stirring swirls, he scooped up a helping. "Drink up."

Ted took the cup and tossed his head back, guzzling the contents with one gulp. After a few seconds, his cheeks puffed out, and he ran for the trees, sick as a cow on alfalfa leaves. Honest-to-Saint Pete, he was just a child.

"You go over there and toss a match on his stomach juice," Curley said. "Bet you a silver dollar it catches fire."

Dill handed me a new cup. I closed my eyes and dumped the offering into my gullet with no more care than Ted had. The drink seared its way into the sour-mash pool of beer I already had sloshing around, but everything stayed put.

"Whoo-hee."

Dill, expectant, hand held out for the return of the cup.

"Not strong enough? What's it need?"

"It needs to be buried ten feet deep."

"Pretty good, huh?"

"Gimme some of it," said Albert, pulling the cup from my grip, bending down to help himself to a serving. He filled his cup to the brim and drank long and deep, like a desert prospector at a miracle spring.

Or maybe one of them old Spanish knights at the fountain of youth.

When he finished, he pretended to pass out by rolling over sideways on the grass with a thud. Always making a commotion. Good ol' Al.

I started laughing again.

Al smacked his lips, loud and fast. "Needs more vinegar."

We all got a kick out of him, and Dill finally got his share, licking his lips and also acting out. Afterwards, we started taking turns at the cup, except for Ted Roberts—who was still off being sick—and Curley.

Near as I could tell, Curley never had so much as a sip of Ol' Bowlegs, but when I paid attention, I saw he was drinking from a brown bottle of his own. He smiled over the three of us like the cat who stole the cream, but his eyes pegged me more often than the others.

I normally hold my liquor sturdy as a cast-iron drum, but Ol' Bowlegs turned more than my knees inside out. Maybe I was nervous from Curley's odd looks.

Either way, after my fourth or fifth swig, the earth got all squishy, and I worked mighty hard to keep it from sliding out away from me. I had a war going with a long-stem thistle plant when Albert threw his arm around my waist and whirled me around toward the front of the woodshed.

"I think the prime has been pumped," he said. "Don't you boys think so?"

Dill tossed back another swallow of Bowlegs.

"What pump ya mean, Kid?"

"I mean August John is oiled up and ready to go."

"What about it, Gus?" Dill said. "You ready to go?"

"Hell, yeah!" My cheer was an involuntary fountain from the guts with no input from the brain. "Where we going?" I had no idea what Dill was talking about or where Al was taking me, but I didn't care.

This was my family. This was my life.

Al spun me around and gave me a shove.

"Inside the shed."

"Insh—insh—in—shide the shed?"

"Scoot, scoot."

I wanted Al to go first. "After you, my . . . good man."

"No, sir. After you."

Okay.

I stepped into the dark, over the door rail onto a hard-packed dirt floor, sniffing out wet maple and hedge wood, dirtdaubers and sagebrush. Something else.

Blinking my eyes in the dark.

I giggled, unsure of myself, unsure of the joke.

The shed was bigger than I realized, more spacious inside. Along with a pile of loose kindling and neat stacks of cut timber, a space was carved out on the north side where a quilt was spread on the ground with pillows. All of this was fuzzy at first, the only sunlight coming in from the open door where Albert stood, blocking my retreat.

All of it stayed fuzzy with the buzzing in my brain.

Then the smells came wafting over again.

Lard and lye soap.

"Howdy, August John."

Propped up in the back corner like a knobby warped fence post, Squeaky disentangled herself from the dark to reach out for me. She was barefoot on the quilt, wearing a flimsy cotton slip.

I remember feeling a crazy rush of familiarity. Of course Squeaky should be here. It seemed like the most natural thing in the world to say *howdy* back.

"How do, Squeaks?"

She put her fingers to my lips, and they were rugged and calloused like a man's.

"S'not very ladylike," I mumbled, but she hushed me again

and stripped off my suit coat fast as cleaning a river trout. She was all business, quiet and deliberate, going for the buttons of my shirt next, while Al just stayed in the doorway, nickering like a horse and fighting off Dill Schiller.

"Let me have a look," Dill said.

"Go 'way, Dill."

"She nekkid is she?"

"Go 'way. Getcha another drink."

Before Squeaky had my third shirt button undone, I had gathered her into my arms for a dance. Two steps toward the pillows, two steps back toward the door. Big spin.

The music was all in my imagination, though I tried to share it through a whistle—unsuccessful.

"You're not so light on your feet, Squeaks."

"A woodshed ain't the place for dancing," she said. Again she was at my buttons.

For some reason, I wanted to dance. The floor was already moving under my feet, and the music wouldn't stop buzzing in my head. It could be Doc hired a band for his wedding, and didn't I see a fiddler up there 'neath the pole barn?

"I'd rather kiss than dance," Squeaky said.

"You think a woodshed's a good place for kissing?"

"I think it's one of the best places for kissing."

Albert spoke up then, his voice coming at me from far down in a well, laced with echoes.

"You get to it, Gus. Let us know when you're done."

"Done? What am I doing?"

The nickering again, and Squeaky pulled open my shirt.

I spun on my bootheel and gazed into her face. Her powder-covered face was ablaze with the afternoon sun, and the rouge circles on her cheeks were bloody red.

The inside of the shed was smothering hot. For a few seconds, I couldn't breathe.

Squeaky grabbed my hand and laced her fingers between mine.

"Ain't you going to kiss me?"

"I surely wonder . . ."

"What? What do you wonder?"

I wondered what in thunder was happening.

"Don't fret none," Squeaky said. "I done a lotta boys their first time. Albert says be gentle with you. I'll be easy as a kitten." She kissed my nose. "I promise you."

Like we'd been hit by a cyclone, the shed pitched sideways. Squeaky still held my shirt and followed me down to the floor with a cluck of her tongue.

Everything spun in a circle, and I tried to stand.

I realized then things were only moving for me.

"I've got to get out of here."

"You need to stay right where you are." She pressed her lips against my neck and started pawing at my belt. I shooed her hand away, my fingers brushing the butt of my gun. Trudy's gun. The one she gave me.

The heat was suffocating, the whirl of the shed wild and uncontrolled.

On one level I knew it was Old Bowlegs making things spin in circles. On another level, I was convinced I was dead and chucked into perdition's flames. Hell is where unfaithful people go, and hadn't I promised my heart to Trudy?

I had?

On the other side of the thin pine-board walls, Albert, Dill, and Curley Grimes were having a fine joke at my expense. I could hear them cackling with filthy glee at my predicament, heard them pouring more hootch into the tub.

Where was all their booze coming from?

Squeaky raked her nails across my bare stomach, and the

goods below my belt tingled in response. "Let's have a kiss, Sweets?"

The smell of her enveloped me. Lard and lye and old lilac perfume. Sweat and musky hair. Whisky and beer and a quilt damp with cat pee.

Her hands navigated with the expertise of a thousand woodshed encounters, and I felt myself respond, slowly but sure. Another minute, I'd be lost.

Another few seconds.

"Don't you go in there."

Curley's voice, deep and insistent. Talking to somebody. Blocking the light from the door.

I tried to sit up, but Squeaky straddled me now, her fingers tracing dirty pictures on my chest, her legs clamping down on my thighs as she tried to unbuckle my belt.

Again, Curley said, "Don't go inside."

"But I saw Gus go inside. I need to talk to—"

I fought to sit up.

"Trudy?"

"Gus?!"

I shoved Squeaky sideways and cried out, "Trudy, get out of here."

But naturally, she was rooted to the spot, catching an eyeful of me without my shirt and Squeaky saddled up like she was busting a bronc. It wasn't like we were indecent, but maybe we were.

I hope I never have to see the kind of expression that washed over Trudy's face. The muscles of her eyes and cheeks and chin went slack. Her color, from pink to gray.

How to describe what I read in those few seconds? Disappointment. Betrayal. Outrage.

Sorrow.

Curley looped an arm around her neck, clamping her in the

crook of his elbow to jerk her sideways. "C'mon, sister, this don't concern you."

She pushed back, kicking, struggling against his rough hold. "Don't you touch me."

Curley handled her like a toy, sweeping her away from the door.

"You let go of her," I said, rolling to my side, desperate to climb to my boots. I reached for my gun, and the damn shed lurched right and left, spilling me onto my butt.

Curley gave Trudy a rough kick in the behind, sending her into a stagger, the blow squeezing my heart. "Get out of here and don't come back, bitch."

I made it up to my hands and knees, fumbled my gun from its holster.

"You . . . rotten . . ."

Curley's boot came down on the floor in front of me. Hard.

"You really want to shoot me, kid?"

"You . . . damn right." I tried to steady the gun with both hands.

"Squeeze the trigger, and every man here will pull iron. There won't be enough of you left over to make chicken scratchin's. Where do you think you are—a sewing bee?"

His words bounced around inside my head, and I knew he was right.

"Trudy."

"She's gone, kid. Get'cha back inside and finish your business."

Outside, Trudy put her hands to her face, hurrying away without looking back, her hair carried on a light breeze. I sobbed and lifted my chin to Curley Grimes.

"I got no business here, you rotten bastard."

Through eyes blurry with tears I saw Curley's massive fist come down and conk me on the jaw. The impact knocked me over on my back.

"He's all yours, Squeaky."

I remember watching a man kill a pig with a sledgehammer once.

This was just like it, and I was the pig.

As I slid into the dark, as I felt Squeaky slide up close to me, I decided to ride with Albert in the morning.

There was nothing left for me in Pleasant Valley.

Chapter Twelve

I woke up inside a bronze cast bell, and my skull was the clapper striking the sides with the power of a steam locomotive.

Clang! Clang! Clang! went the inside of my head. I opened my eyes behind the flat-topped woodshed afraid I was going to die. After trying to stand up, I was afraid I wouldn't.

Crawling over to the shed, I used its gnarly wall to pull myself to my boots. I couldn't regain my balance. I caught two splinters deep in my fingers doing it. One more thing sore as hell.

Clang! Clang! Clang!

Bird song is all it was, a field sparrow welcoming the red dawn, but Ol' Bowlegs had every twitter of his beak sounding like cymbals in a brass band. Or a marble slamming around inside a tin can. My tongue was a dead gopher, the roof of my mouth a cement urn.

I was warmed over mud with low spirits to match.

After a while, Albert found me leaning against the back of the shed. He tried to scrub me out with fresh coffee and toast, nothing staying down for long. After a while he hoisted me onto a liver chestnut with white stockings, and we rode a trail west away from Richardson's place with the sun cooking our backs. Al had tied a bedroll to my horse. A canteen hung off the saddle horn, and a coil of rope.

I didn't so much as bother to ask where we were going.

Away.

Someplace else.

Not Pleasant Valley or Morris's Crossing.

East.

He led us onto the wide sprawl of Nebraska, just the two of us following the whim of his nature. I clenched my jaw tight, warring against the crash and bang every clop of the trail shot through my head. "How about we go to some glorious place we can be Kid Wade and August John without a care in the world?"

My gun was back in its holster, poking my leg, but I didn't recall putting it there.

Them splinters in my hand swelled up red and festering.

The two of us crossed up from the Niobrara to the choppy landscape of the Keya Paha. Albert trotting along, jaw set, back straight, wearing a clean long-sleeved buckskin shirt, me slogging along behind, head thumping like a Ponca Indian powwow.

By and by, I felt some better. After an hour or so, I had enough energy to put together a thought.

"What about Black George and Dill?" I said. "Aren't they riding along with us?" It hadn't occurred to me to ask about anybody else, but now the floodgate of memory was open from the night before, most of it stinking like raw sewage. I remember Al saying we'd take a run for some horses.

"I didn't think we'd need those fellas on this run, after all," Al said. "For now, we'll go it alone."

The sun came up over the horizon like somebody pitched a hot rock straight up. It had a weird crimson tint, and the sky was copper green like an old penny. I thought about Trudy's boose stories and the waspers and monsters of the Niobrara, because it felt eerie quiet.

Later we saw storm clouds, long and stretched out at the foot of the sky, billowing up tall, threatening afternoon rain or hail. Al said, "The blasted weather's got a hard-on for us."

We cleared a high crest, and my head cleared like pulling a drain plug.

It was the kind of day it was.

One summer, I saw hail in the Sandhills so thick it covered the ground like snow. I hoped I wouldn't see such a thing today without a slicker. I double-checked to see if Al had maybe brought one along for me, but he had not.

We watched a raccoon trundle across the road in broad daylight. Albert shot it straight through the gizzard, but not without a scolding. "See what happens when you come in late from a night on the town?"

The dead coon rolled through the dust like an oak barrel.

I said, "If you come in after daylight, folks figure you're crazy sick and blow your brains out."

Al agreed. "Let it be a lesson to all of us, Gus."

Well, I guess that old raccoon was asking for it being out in the daylight.

Now recalling what happened at the wedding party the night before, I stewed over Trudy in my head, calling myself names, realizing what a rat I had been. I wasn't the only one.

Just before we stopped to water the horses, I rode up close to Albert.

"Got a question for you."

"Ask me anything."

"Me and Squeaky."

"You and Squeaky. There's a romance if ever was one."

"Did we . . . I mean, after Trudy was there. I remember Curley hit me."

"You oughtn't call Curley names. But he knows you were drunk, and he'll forgive you."

"Doesn't matter. I want to know if me and Squeaky . . . got together."

"What if I said you did?"

"I'd hate your guts for setting it up."

"What if I said you didn't?"

"I guess I'd hate your guts the same."

"You've got to give me a vested interest in telling the truth, son. Otherwise, how can I answer your question?"

"How about you just say what happened? How about you tell me the truth because it's the right thing to do?"

"Ain't no such thing." He picked at his nose and flicked a crusty wad of snot across the plains.

I tried going at him from a different direction.

"You want me riding at your back if I'm carrying a grudge?"

"If you're trying to tell me about your gun, I already saw it up close. Ol' Curley showed it to us last night. Nice rig—Trudy set you up fine."

"Did you hear what I said?"

"Take it easy, boy. You want the truth about Squeaky? Here it is. It just so happens you didn't wake up after Curley's tap. Slept straight through until this morning, and Squeaky had better money to be made elsewhere."

"So we didn't do anything?"

"I think she checked in and tucked up your quilt around midnight."

I felt a flow of gratitude flush through me. Good ol' Squeaky.

"She's a right fine gal underneath it all," I said.

Al's voice was firm. "No. She's not a fine gal at all."

"I hate leaving Trudy like this."

"You shouldn't."

"I let her down. We came to the wedding together. Doc said I should look after Betty."

"Who's Betty?"

I told him about the cow and calf.

"She can keep track of her own damn cow. She was doing it before you happened along, and she'll be fine without you. And

Doc be damned."

I wondered if Doc and Al had a falling out. He kept talking, so I didn't say a word.

"This horse run is just what you need, right now, Gus. Give yourself some time to calm down. Get your head on straight."

"I think I oughta be back home."

Al reined his horse in to a stop. "Home? What home?"

I felt my face flush red. "I guess I started thinking of Pleasant Valley as my home."

"Men like us ain't got no home. 'Specially not there."

"Pleasant Valley's a nice spread."

"Pleasant Valley is spoiled. The old man seen to it."

"You're talking about your dad?"

Al turned his faith toward the sky. "Goddamn, it's a beautiful day."

"Stormy day."

We sat there awhile, quiet, not saying a word. Finally, Al clucked his horse along the trail. "We got a lot of miles to cover, best be moving."

"Trudy told me about your dad. I mean, about him and her."

"Trudy's full of horse apples, if you don't mind me saying so."

I thought he was done, but he kept on with the line of thought.

"And if you do mind me saying it, I'll yank ya off your horse—which is my horse—and stomp you with a boot. Sound good?"

For the first time in a long time, I couldn't tell if he was joking or not, and I saw the Lightning in its holster was buttoned back onto his belt.

"Let's not talk about Trudy or my old man, either one," Al said.

"I showed Trudy where we found Boots and Windy."

"What of it?"

"They weren't there anymore. Somebody must've dragged 'em away."

"Coyotes likely."

"You studied any more on who might've had it in for them?"

No word from Al in response.

Okay, we'd be quiet.

When I realized I had no idea where we were, I thought we should stop and make a plan. We continued to parallel the great shallow slash of the river. But for how long? Al was a good thirty feet in front of me, and I called out.

"I do believe we're traveling away from the Indians."

He waved his left hand without looking back, so I rode up on him, and we talked awhile.

"Ain't we going for Sioux horses? When were you planning to turn north?" I knew I was burr headed because of all the booze in my system. But I knew my directions. Without a keen sense of direction, you get lost real quick in this country, and I was feeling pretty flushed out anyway.

We hadn't hit the area around Niobrara City for many moons, but we weren't taking the usual trail to get there.

Al loved to keep me guessing. It was like a game he played with people, but I thought he cared enough about me not to do it.

Maybe the horse run was another crazy game. It's what our whole entire life was turning into.

Noontime, and we traveled south and east along the Niobrara, back toward our childhood homes.

In a little ravine close to Paddock, we ate pig sandwiches leftover from Doc's wedding. Then we pushed farther along with the sun settling in behind us.

"I guess I figured to forego the Indian horses for this go-round."

"You guess? You figured?"

"Just clam up a minute and see what I see."

"Well—okay." I followed his outstretched arm with my eyes and saw him pointing at a small corral standing in the middle of nowhere. The corral was empty, but behind it on the open range were a ten-count of horses. Red duns and grullas with satin black manes and heavy brush tails. Notched ears and a brand on every hip. I squinted my eyes nearly shut but couldn't make out the mark.

The closer we rode to the horses, the more nervous they became. One of the lead mares broke off from the rest and started prancing around, blowing fire and brimstone from her nostrils. Another one bulled through the herd the opposite way.

I was nervous, scared nervous, with my imagination doing somersaults into the dark because it was notch-eared horses Boots and Windy took. "Look where it got them taking horses from locals," and of course it wasn't them at all who took the horses to begin with, but it wasn't always sitting well with me to see Albert in direct sunlight.

"Boots and Windy's horses were buckskins," Albert said, like it made all the difference in the world.

"Maybe so." I decided to argue with him. And I didn't like to argue with him. "Remember what Doc said about dogs and messing up your own backyard, and—"

"And we're five thousand miles from your backyard. Nobody out here knows us."

"Doc's well known around Paddock."

"Doc is pretty well known everywhere from here to Texas. You and me are not."

I wasn't sure about it, and I told him so, my voice shaky enough to touch his heart maybe because he said, "Look, if it will make you feel better, we'll collect up a couple and turn 'em around today for some hard, fast money. Two horses in the entire world are gonna make no difference at all."

I thought he might be right. He was always sounding right. Even then, after what happened with Squeaky and Trudy. He still sounded right. I wanted it so badly for him to be right.

Two horses, twelve. Twelve hundred.

We were specks really, all of us nothing more than a couple pinpricks on the colossal expanse of unorganized territory west. Like ticks on an immense hide covering millions and millions of acres, insects among miniscule colonies of other ticks, and what difference did one or two specks make? It was odd, but I suddenly felt it as true as anything, and it made everything Albert did right.

"As long as we turn 'em around today," I said.

Uncoiling a snappy lariat with a tough rawhide honda, Al had a loop sizzling through the air above his head quick as snake spit. "We might snub the blowhard up to my roan to break her," he said. From the way she moved, she weren't no bronc, but Al liked playing cowboy.

Slippery Jack in action.

"You go toward the fence; I'll scoot on around."

A fast-action move we'd used before to peel a critter off from the others.

I was happy he hadn't asked me to snub the mare to my chestnut. She and I had got to know each other pretty well. We had come to a good understanding, but I'd'a felt bad putting her through the paces. And I wasn't looking forward to working the rope. Those slivers I acquired in my fingers early in the morning were boiled up something fierce.

The gaucho-ear mare saw me coming on the chestnut and swung into Al's oncoming rush. She was a pretty grulla with sweet supple muscles and smooth flanks like taffy, but she had a spooky look in her eyes.

Al dropped the rope over her head nice and easy as you

please. Wouldn't you know she pulled up fast and stopped without a fight, heaving in and out like a bellows.

I didn't like the look of her but came close enough to examine the burn on her butt. "You recognize the brand? Looks like a drunken *K*."

"*K* for Clausen."

"Clausen? Way out here?"

"Shoot, yes. The old peckerwood's such a big shot, I thought he'd appreciate donating to charity." I laughed at Al calling him peckerwood.

"Clausen really does think he's hot shit on a silver platter."

"Cold turds on a grass mat," Albert said. "How about you take this horse, and I'll bring along another one?"

"I'd rather you take her, and I catch another one." The expression on the mare's face was like a dozen spiders skittering around my neck. She scared hell out of me.

"Go ahead, then. You got the better rope anyway," Al said.

It took me the better part of fifteen minutes to pull in a horse. First, they'd tear the ground off one way, then fire back toward the far and wide. The chestnut was doing her best to show off for me—I think she wanted to do well. I hated to take advantage, so I let a gorgeous gelding skip right past.

Finally, we picked up another mare, smaller than Albert's, a red dun with a more friendly air about her. She didn't seem to mind the hemp I put on her. Almost like she'd been yearning for a good reason to get up and go see some new country. Well, here were me and Al happy to oblige her, leading the two prize treasures back into the West.

My new gal settled in nicely behind the chestnut for the walk.

"Let's take these," Al said.

"Why not?"

"There's a couple homesteads we passed earlier. We can swap these girls quick."

The way he talked, I think he had it all figured out ahead of time. Maybe as far back as when we left Richardson's ranch. I'll never know.

"If we're lucky, maybe we'll get supper out of the deal," Al said.

I followed him for an hour, sucking at the sore slivers in my fingers, as winds pushed up clouds in the east until a sandy patch of ground turned into a cow trail, the cow trail turning into a road. "All roads lead to Rome," he said. "You ever heared it?"

"No. What's it mean?"

"Means money always wins in the end." I didn't think what he said was right, but I couldn't think of a better explanation.

At the end of the road, a house rose up ahead of us, a sugar cube against a shadow-blue canvas cloud. Sure of itself, plunked on the barren earth without any trees.

Smug, like there would never be wind to bother it. Defiant like it was the last house at the end of the world.

We kept walking, and it grew larger in the blood-red evening.

Chapter Thirteen

The homestead was more farm than ranch, a family affair tied together with a string of brawny offspring, six or seven of them male. The girls were just as wide at the shoulder as the boys, but they wore their curly hair long. I told Al it's the only way I could tell them apart.

The patriarch of this Bohemian acreage was called Cyril Cernek. The wife was Tilda. They'd come across on the boat from the Old Country back in '72, barely speaking English.

Their accents were so thick, any normal body would be hard pressed to understand 'em, but Al and me grew up around Bohemians, so it wasn't a problem.

The whole thing was fantastic with King Cyril bossing around these boys the entire time we were there. "Fetch beers from the cellar," and "Did ya check on the boar pigs?" and "Get our company a nice pair of chairs to rest in."

Plopped down in the middle of a settler's purgatory of scratching and scraping at drought-ridden sod and grasshopper-chewed crops, The Cernek prosperity was as much a surprise to Al as it was to me.

"Ya, and ya got some purty horses," said the old man.

"Our luck is running true," I told Al when nobody was paying attention.

"You don't think I didn't know about the old Czech?"

But he didn't. Not before we rode in on them.

Inside the kitchen flies landed everywhere, swirling around

the corner slop bucket, and one of the little girls marched around with a wire and paper flyswatter. *Whap!*

Tilda made coffee bitter thick with clouds of heavy whipping cream, served up by older big-muscled girls in tiny china cups. We sat around a table big as a buckboard wagon.

Al said we were cowboys looking for work. We'd seen their place and ventured in for a drink. Cyril said we were welcome to hear all about his adventures.

Sipping coffee, munching little vanilla cookies, watching flies meet their maker, Al asked, "Came right over from the mother country did you?"

"The smell of wildflowers. The taste of fresh apples. America called to me in a dream," Cyril said.

I guess it was true, because I've had similar dreams where I tasted a plug of tobacco or smelled a skunk.

After dawdling around, going broke for a spell in Iowa, Cyril decided to try further west in Nebraska.

The Cerneks were set up real nice, with a house big as a castle and acres of pasture ground packed crazy with cows and pigs and rows of corn. With all them husky boys to work, I figured Cyril had life set up in front of him like a fancy Sunday dinner.

"You'll stay for supper of course."

The little mercenary crushed a fly on the table and flicked it down to the floor where she reveled in mashing it under her shoe.

She was having fun, so Cyril walked us around the house and garden, and we smoked fat black cigars.

"You boys ought to watch yourselves traveling alone."

"We know the country well enough," I said.

"Ya, and I see your fancy shooters." It might've been my imagination. My stomach was empty as a cat's conscience, but Cyril's voice had what you might call an ominous tone when he cast an eye toward our new horses. "Still ya might want'a be careful. Vigs have been known to be running about these parts." He caught Al offguard.

"Vigs? Oh, you mean vigilantes."

"Ya, and there's vigilance committees all up and down the river as I hear it."

"I never heard of such a thing."

"Next you'll tell me you ain't selling those hayburners ya got there."

"As it turns out, the grulla and dun are for sale, yes, sir."

"I figured ya for scalpers or salesmen of some kind. My advice is to make tracks out of this country." Cyril shook his head. "Better days in the future. Someplace else."

Al's features froze into a half scowl, and his gaze shifted back and forth between me and the old man.

One of the boys, Frank Cernek, rang the chuckwagon triangle then, and we had no choice but to step back into the kitchen to a spread like I'd never seen. The sensuous warm smells smoothed us out, and Al was the first to drop his hat under the table and say pass the potatoes.

But it wasn't so simple.

Chafing to dig in, we straddled our chairs, forced to wait while Cyril ran us through a long-ass sermon about being thankful for the bounty and how we had to cross ourselves three times before feeding our faces, and wasn't it right and proper to invite Jesus, Mary, and the Holy Ghost to dine with us?

I didn't care if they let the flies get their share as long as I could get started.

After the amens, we still couldn't eat as platters stacked with ham and pitchers of lemonade and soft cistern water went 'round and 'round between the two immigrants and a dozen kids. Pass the bowl of green beans and bacon, take a bite, watch the bread, the corn, the slaw come around. Better take a scoop for yourself before one of the hulking blond boys cleaned things out.

I sat beside a bruiser called Paul, who had a harelip running from his nose down to his curlicue mouth, and who pestered me for anything on my plate not getting rapid attention. "Ya gonna eat your onion? Don't you want your beans?" But he was too big to elbow in the ribs.

I finished my lemonade—the best I ever tasted, sour-sweet, and Tilda Cernek said it had sprigs of mint in it, what I thought were lemon-tree leaves.

"The glasses are from Boheme, the capitol of my home place, and they came over on the boat with my brother Tad."

Albert swore his family had an identical set.

Cyril forked down a wedge of liver while swallowing a spoon of corn, and I pictured a ship big as three cottonwood trees lugging everybody's glass across the water.

Across the table from Al, Paul's brother Frank, red haired and freckled, kept smirking down at him, like maybe he had the same suspicions about us as old Cyril.

It was past time to get lost, but the raisin pie and fresh whipped cream came out next. The little hellion was back up, spiraling around the table like a drain, smacking flies into oblivion. With every slap of the swatter Cyril or Al or one of the giant brothers would belch with satisfaction.

Finally, Frank broke his silence. "Them horses outside got an interesting brand on 'em."

"Indeed they do," Albert agreed. "Picked 'em up for a song from a musician I know. A horn blower who plays at the opera houses in Iowa. Maybe you've heard of him?"

"I don't think so."

"He's a foreigner, an immigrant like yourselves is why I asked."

Frank shook his head, half smiling now. He knew Al was

teasing him, but he was at least two or three years older than us and twice as big. Twice as much *everything.*

He didn't care if he was teased.

Damn, damn, damn. I knew where this was going, and I prayed he would shut up.

Al ignored me as I stood up from my place at the table. I wiped my lips with my sleeve.

"We better ride on out. We've still got a lot of ground to cover."

Cyril patted his lips with his napkin and tossed it onto his plate. Without bothering to rise, he said, "Ya, you better be on your way." I think he saw trouble brewing between Al and Frank.

"Thank you for the meal, ma'am," I said, nodding to Tilda and the girls.

"You're sure you don't know any immigrant horn blowers?" Al asked Frank.

I dropped my hand down hard on his shoulder and squeezed. "Al, we need to go." He shrugged my hand aside.

Al might've thought he was playing with the fellow, but Frank was giving as good as he got. "What is the name of this horn player you got the horses from?"

Every time Al hooked a fish, he grinned the same cold, awful way. But I thought this fish was a shark, and I was ready to get clear of the water.

No way to warn Al in time. He delivered the punchline.

"Like I say, this musician, he's from the old country. Just like you." Al stuck out his chin and looked down his nose at Frank. "I think his name is Kissa Myass."

All the hustle and bustle of the kitchen stopped. The flies quit swarming, and the hell-child dropped her flyswatter.

Al bent down to retrieve his hat, his eye locked expectantly on Frank, his crooked grin twitching under his nose. Then he pushed himself away from the table and stood up next to me.

Putting on his hat, he gave the family a two-fingered salute at the brim. "Be seeing ya."

He shooed me out of the house ahead of him, walking backwards toward the door, keeping his eye on the table.

Once we were out, he ran for his horse, whooping and whistling. I did my best to keep up as he leapt on his roan and led his grulla up the lane in a cloud of dust, hollering obscene insults back to the good people who had fed us.

Glancing over my shoulder, I saw Cyril standing in the doorway, watching us ride into the dusky night, and lightning traced an outline around the house in the clouds behind.

Just after dark, we tried to sell the horses in a roadhouse along Ponca Creek, but nobody was buying. There were three men inside—one did most of the talking, the one with the biggest belly. He had thick black hair and a beard and talked like a mush-mouth but wouldn't shut up for love nor money. His buddies were dumb as rocks, nodding at every little thing Blackbeard spat out including how they were scared of the Sioux now with those ranchers being killed. Seems like the story was spreading like fire all up and down the river.

The place was only about a mile from Old Baldy where I grew up, but I didn't know any of the men. It's where the town of Lynch is today, which I guess tells you something about what we could expect.

Al's temper had been on a slow boil ever since Cyril the Bohonk got all high and mighty with us, so Blackbeard's refusal to so much as put an eye to our horses fried him to the bone.

Plus, when we came back outside to the trail, it finally started raining.

"See what we have to put up with?" Al said. "See the pig slop we deal with day in and day out?"

He turned on me, water falling from his hat onto his

shoulders. When he shook his finger, flicks of rain flew at my face. Tiny liquid bullets but with the wallop of a prize fighter behind 'em.

Prize loud mouth was more like it.

It was all so amazing and ridiculous. Al standing there in the rain, ranting and raving and stomping in the mud because these three old badgers wouldn't come outside in a rainstorm to give Al money for strange horses. It was clear from the looks on their faces they figured the horses were stolen.

"All them sumbucks want to do is lay around in their own filth and get drunk."

"Looks the same to me," I said, agreeing with him. What else could I do? He was twisting in the wind, and I didn't want him to turn his temper on me.

"I don't have to do this, ya know. I could be down to Council Bluffs working for the damn railroad or running a river barge or just about any damn thing."

"I know you could."

"No reason I should take this kind of abuse."

"Nope."

"I got half a mind to go back inside there and shoot the place up."

"Waste of bullets."

"You think so? I ain't so sure." Much to my relief, he didn't touch his gun but instead walked over to my chestnut horse and untied the lead rope I had strung over to the red dun. Tossing down the hemp and making sure to stomp on the end as it fell, he then went to set the stolen grulla free.

"What'cha doing, Al?"

"Hell, I'm just gonna turn 'em loose. What's the point of draggin' 'em along through a stinkin' rainstorm? Nobody wants 'em. It ain't like the old days. No, sir."

He spun around on his heel like a kid's top and started hollering at the top of his lungs to scare the Clausen horses away. "Yah, yah, yah."

The grulla took a single step back, eyeing Al like he was out of his skull. The red dun flung her head sideways, equally perplexed.

"Go on, ya fleabag old nags. Get out of here."

It suddenly occurred to me this was maybe what Blackbeard had intended for Al to do. Maybe he'd given us the cold shoulder hoping we'd come out and set the animals free rather than deal with them in the rain.

But no, as Al spun around, slipping and sliding, waving his arms and burning his anger, I decided it was giving the lazy men too much credit. They weren't so cagey.

"Run, ya mangy piece of fly bait!"

I pulled my horse around to follow Al as he finally got the Clausen horses moving. We wandered into the dark.

Al ran and ran through the rain ahead of me and the two horses, which I dutifully led along through the torrent, my hat bowed down against the cold and wet. Splashing, splashing, splashing, he was staying far ahead. I saw him when the clouds flashed with lightning, a black blob bouncing, bouncing, bouncing, still running, though the horses had long since veered away across the open range.

It would take him a while to lose his anger. It was taking longer each time. Longer than it used to.

"You're being a good friend to him," I told myself, but maybe I wasn't so certain.

I sure wished I was warm in my barn stall at Pleasant Valley, tending Betty and listening to Trudy tell boose stories. Might welcome some Bible reading, let her run me through a few begats. That's how bad it was.

Albert cried in the night, and I thought there was nobody to hear him.

"Yaaaaaahhhhhhh."

Lightning flashed, and I saw we were at the foot of Old Baldy, the towering windswept rock formation I visited so often as a kid. Back then the stark-naked stone surrounded by its slight tree line and so much brush made me feel grounded. We were on the Missouri River bluffs.

The Indians said Old Baldy contained magic inside to cure disease.

If I ever needed curing, now was the time. Soaked through, lonesome, I stared at the pale beige rock, and with every burst of silver light, I held fast to an afterimage in the dark.

It was magnificent.

So busy waiting for another glimpse of the rock, I didn't notice the four riders on horseback.

Not until they were already on top of me, bashing my brains out.

Chapter Fourteen

Anybody who's ever been in a fight knows half of what me and Albert went through in front of Old Baldy in the rain.

Half—because most folks get a chance to hit back, whereas I was only hoping for a chance to stay alive. There wasn't any fighting back. Just grit your teeth (what was left of them) and take it.

It might not have been as bad on a clear night without the rain, but the slimy dogs didn't play fair sneaking in on us out of the dark. And it wasn't Blackbeard and his skinny friends, which is what I first thought, because they didn't have anything against us.

Not like Freckle-face the Bohonk who Al told to "kiss-my-ass" and who got so mad he pulled his pals or brothers or whoever it was with him out into the rain to follow us.

I recognized his voice right away after the first rider swung in and separated me from my chestnut. "I get first shot at this thievin' plug-sucker," said Freckle-face. I remembered his name was Frank just before he planted his boot heel in my face.

I collapsed like an empty gunny sack. On the plus side, the slivers in my fingers didn't bother me anymore. Not much at all.

My dinner companion, Paul Cernek—the big one with the harelip—hit next, slamming his toes into my ribs. I rolled with the kick, picking up a ton of mud, maybe saving my ribs from breaking. For all the good it did as another guy dropped a knee onto my chest, stopping my heart. No way to breathe, I tossed both arms up over my face, tried to pull my knees up for protection as another volley of blows hit my shoulders, my chin, my legs.

The rain came down hard, but when the sky lit up again, I thought it was Albert, flashing explosive powder-smoke, punching holes in these boys. Filling them with lead.

Sadly, it was only more thunder. Al wasn't coming to the rescue. The only punching being done was by three big boys smelling of liver and lemonade breath, their cackles and oaths running together in my head, a continuous roar.

My gun fell from its holster, and, God's grace, wouldn't you know big Frank was kind enough to pick it up. He spun the cylinder in the sky above my face and poked the barrel up under my nose. "Our family, we don't take any guff off a no horse thieves. We just practice the Three-*S* Rule. You all know what the Three-*S* Rule is, don't you, boy?"

When Frank crashed the steel gun muzzle through my top front teeth, I went a little gray, waking up enough to hear, "Shoot, shovel, and shut-the-hell-up."

"Aw, Frank, it's like pluggin' a kitten."

"I plugged a passel of sick kittens in my time."

"I know, but I ain't got no shovel."

"Paul's right," said the third boy, whose name I never learned. "We leave his body out here, somebody's bound to find it, and Pa don't like no questions. Questions lead to trouble."

"Vigs wouldn't give a shit. Vigs would stretch this possum-lover's neck and let the crows eat his eyeballs."

"Vigs don't answer to Pa. I just don't want to deal with his stupid carcass in the rain."

I got to admit I was tremblin' like never before as blood washed down my throat and chin, and every ounce of energy I had was focused on staying awake. If I was gonna be killed, I wanted to see it firsthand.

For his part, Frank felt conflicted. I could appreciate that.

"I don't know if I should kill you or just leave you in misery. What do you have to say for yourself, thief?"

"W-we . . . didn't mean . . . no ill will."

"Speak for yourself. Your pal's a rude little bastard."

"I . . . am speakin' for myself."

"Thought you pink-bellied worms stuck together."

"Al's . . . a . . . corker."

"A corker? Hell, yes. You say his name's Al?"

"Albert," I whimpered. I admit, I whimpered. Anybody would whimper with their skull broke in two and their kidneys turned to corn mush.

"Albert?" The rain came down in curtains behind Frank's shadow as he stood over top of me, but he seemed to be wavering, so, mostly just to waste more time, I kept talking.

"Albert Wade."

"Kid Wade? Not the Kid? Slippery Jack?"

"Same. We . . . we didn't mean no harm."

"Hey, Frank, the Kid rides with Middleton."

"Shit," said Frank, the revelation stirring something up in his guts. Maybe he wasn't such a tough guy anymore. "Okay. Shit."

He tossed my gun down into the mud beside me.

"Get over there and make sure Samuel hasn't killed him already."

Mention Doc's name, and, just like snapping my fingers, the bully sons of Cyril Cernek were gone, leaving me a pain-racked bleeding wreck, half drowned in mud, coughing up my teeth, praying they stopped this other boy from killing Albert.

And the next morning, I couldn't move. Not an inch. But the sky was blue and crystal clear high above. When I didn't see any buzzards circling overhead, I took it as a good sign.

When the gray wisps of cloud cleared from my mind and the screaming rush of blood and agony finally died away inside my ears, I opened my eyes. Twenty-four hours before, my head was stuffy with drink. Now my entire body was held in a vise. I can't remember ever feeling worse. Ever before, or any time since.

Every muscle was like winter cast iron, cold and brittle. The marrow of my bones ached. My skin was torn and cut and split open in a dozen spots, and crusted blood filled the top of my mouth where air whistled through a gap in my teeth.

My hair hurt.

I lay for most of an hour in a puddle of rain, not knowing if I'd wet myself or if I was so drenched the sun simply refused to reach down and dry me. Finally, the cramps forced me to reposition myself. It took everything I had to lift my body into a seated position before politely tipping over again.

This was all going to take some time.

My new angle had me facing away from the sun, and, down the trail a ways, I saw a bump in the road squirming every now and then.

Albert!

Then it was true—they got him just like me.

I went a little crazy then with worry for Al, but at the same time I hadn't seen any horses, and we were a long way from any place, in no condition to walk. If those stupid horses wandered off, I was gonna really get mad. The sandy insides of my cheeks and granite-dry throat told me I needed water—bad. Nobody healed up with dirty mud puddles to drink. Another night outside, I might die. At least, those were the thoughts that went slinging through my brain like whips of thread on a loom, weaving out a tapestry of pure-dee horror.

"A-al-berrrt!" If my voice sounded loud in my head, it was probably only above a whisper in real life. He didn't so much as twitch. Maybe he was dead already.

After forever, I got on top of my boots and dragged myself ten miles to him—maybe forty feet. Truth to tell, battered a little bit and bruised up, he looked a lot better than I felt. He'd only had one of the devils whipping him, while I had three.

No fair at all. Why?

"I'll bet they thought I was you," I said out loud. "In the dark, they couldn't tell who was who. It was your clever mouth got us in dutch, and my corpse paid the tab." I gotta say, I almost kicked him a good one just lying there.

Instead, I turned my head side to side. Working the kinks out, my neck didn't hurt as bad as it did when I first came to, and scanning the landscape netted a view of two horses grazing a stone's throw away—the liver chestnut and Al's roan.

We were saved.

I nudged Al in the side with the toe of my boot. He turned his head and squinted up at me with one eye. "Wha?"

I must've looked like the old reaper of death all slumped over with blood dried on my chin and down my shirt. Albert jumped three feet high onto his feet and scampered back like a slapped pup.

Once't he saw it was me, he cupped his knees in his hands and bent over with relief, the sides of his rib cage puffing in and out. "Lord a'mighty, you scared me, Gus."

Right off I could see he was in better shape than me, hardly a scratch on 'im for all the rumpled clothes and a big red bruise on his cheekbone. I could've wished at least a broken nose or cracked rib, but the smart aleck got off with horse feathers.

"I need a drink," I said. "Got . . . pretty busted up."

"Aw, you'll be all right." He touched the tender part of his face. "Holy cow, what a slug I took."

"You took?"

He turned his face to me like he was trying out for a play-actor's part on the stage. "Sure, take a look-see. Is it real bad?"

"You look a lot better than I feel."

"Yeah, yeah." He continued to poke at his cheek. "How about you grab the horses, will ya?"

Right about then I couldn't grab my elbow without throwing up. The world spun like a wheel, and I was the hub. "I . . . think somebody forgot to grease the bearings . . ."

"What nonsense are you talking? Gus? Gus!"

I didn't hear anything he said until the pain in my ribs was so great, I had to scream in Al's face.

Halfway up the barrel of the chestnut, I caught him hoisting me into the saddle.

"Just hold onto the horn, ya sheepherder. Once y'r in place, we can ride."

I understood, if vaguely, what he wanted me to do. Every part of me was sore, but every part of me wanted to get off the wide high country and crawl into a cozy hole to lick my wounds. Riding off on the chestnut was the best way to do it, so I played along, but it took every piece of grit I ever had.

Satisfied I was seated properly, Al climbed up onto his roan.

"You think you're 'wake enough to hold onto the reins?"

"Sure thing."

"Because if you're not, I'll have to leave you here and bring back help."

"Or carry me on your horse."

"I'm not so sure . . ."

My suggestion didn't set well with him so I waved him off. "I'll be . . . good. I'll be good."

The first three miles were excruciating.

Eventually, I got situated on the leather, and the familiar rhythm had me lulled to rest. Like I always said about the chestnut, he was one of the best mounts I ever rode. We hit it off like bread and jam. He had a sense of my hurt, seemed extra careful where he put his hooves down. It might seem silly or like some of Trudy's weirdy stuff, but I think critters have special knowledge we don't understand, can feel things and sense things more than we can. I think my horse was a sensitive, tender fellow—which sounds like the kind of thing a girl would say.

We rode until dark, looping south, making a wide curve around Paddock, halfway to the Elkhorn River, then came back up along Eagle Creek to make camp for the night. Along the way, Al shot at a couple rabbits and hit one—so we'd have supper. Just thinking about it lifted my spirits.

When we stopped, Al gave me a choice between tending to the horses or cleaning the rabbit and building a fire.

"If you don't want to bother with the rabbit, we can have a cold camp," he said. I couldn't imagine what he was thinking. Let our rabbit go to the coyotes?

But I think he was concerned about drawing unwanted attention.

"I'm hungry enough to eat him raw, but I figure Mr. Long Ears will taste better if we roast him up."

"Whatever you think."

When he pulled a short canvas sack from under his saddle blanket, I said, "What's this now?"

"Grain for the horses." It wasn't more than five or ten pounds. Not much for them to burn, and we were fortunate in having a lush spring with tall forage around the cricks. The sack of feed was horse dessert.

"Where did you get such a supply?" I knew we hadn't picked it up before we took on the drunken-*K* horses but couldn't think of any time Al had been out of my sight.

"The Cernek brothers had it along. I wasn't sure what was in it."

I sat down beside my pile of kindling to sort out what he was saying.

"Ouch."

"You sure you're all right, August John? You don't need me to set a bone or something?"

"I'll be fine."

"Because, I set a bone once't for my ma. She slipped on the ice hauling water, and—"

"Look, I said I'm fine. I'm just trying to imagine you whistling 'Dixie,' shopping for dry goods in the middle of a lightning storm while I'm getting kicked to hell by those Bohemian boys."

"Wasn't like you say at all."

"What was it like then?"

"Big flash of lightning, and I saw this canvas sack hanging from ol' Paul Cernek's saddle. They were distracted with you, so I snapped it up. I was hoping it was gold coin." He poured it on the ground in front of our two saddle pals. The horses eagerly buried their nose in the pile.

Disappointed and pouting, he dusted his hands. "It's nothing but oats."

He'd seen the sack hanging from Cernek's saddle. Instead of coming to the aid of a friend, he went for the sack, gambling on the chance of reward.

He couldn't help himself.

I was about to make a smart aleck remark when something new caught my eye. I nodded off to his right, and Al followed the direction indicated.

"I'll be a son of a gun," he said. "It's them two drunken-*K* horses again."

The grulla and the dun seemed bashful at the approach, but it was clear they had followed us on our meandering trek across the territory. "Come on, Gus—help me round 'em up."

It took every ounce of strength I had to stand up and join him, but, once I got to moving, I realized I was more stove up from the saddle than truly injured from the previous night's fight. Far as I could tell, I'd told Al true and didn't have any broken bones.

Except my mouth, and it still hurt like hell and would for the next week or so, especially when I drank cold spring water.

After we got the drunken-*K* horses hobbled close to our trotters, I finally got back to making a fire.

Al found a few good sticks to make a spit.

Within an hour we were chewing fried rabbit hide like it was a fine delicacy. In some places over in Europe it is, but they usually have gravy and dumplings or something.

Al licked his fingers and lay back on his rolled-up blanket. "Nothing like last night's spread, but it'll do."

"The Cerneks set a good table, but I don't like the cost. Makes me angry I put a dime under the plate when we left."

"You didn't." Al was incredulous. "You left a dime for the grub?"

"Shoot, yes. You were too busy insulting our host to notice."

"Your foolhardy head's gonna lead you to the poorhouse, Gus. You mark my words."

"Yeah, yeah."

I'd had enough conversation for a while and sank back on my own blanket—gingerly. After I tipped my hat down over my eyes, I believe I fell asleep for a spell. The contented sound of horses munching, the trickle of the crick, the crackle of the fire, and the warmth it provided on my left side carried me deep into slumber before I knew it.

I woke up gently to Al's diatribe about Trudy.

"She's a fair thing—fairly helpless. But innocent, and pretty enough in a plain sort of way. You know what stops her from being downright homely is her hair. There's a nice, natural curl there sort of saves her looks. I hate to think what another ten years will put on her. You listening to me, Gus?"

"She was good enough for you to kiss on."

"Aw, she's my cousin. What else can I do?"

"You carry on like a horny old dog with all your cousins?"

"She's available is all." He stretched his arms and I made myself more comfortable.

Above us, the stars popped into life, a million million of them. Al matched 'em with as many words.

"I s'spect one of these days somebody will settle there in Pleasant Valley, sort of like you were saying the other day, but I guess you got more sense than to follow up on such a dumb thing. I mean, the place is all right as far as it goes. I'm not so overly excited about it. One of these days somebody will hook up with old Trudy. Knock out a couple pups. Maybe old man Clausen. Like I say, she's not much of a looker."

"Says you," I murmured. Then, after a few heartbeats, "Be good if she quit dealing in guns."

"And damn if you ain't spot on saying it," Al said. "I told her so, but she don't listen to me."

"Mmm-hmmm."

"She sure does need to be careful. Once Doc gets over acting all lovey-dovey with Pood, we can all be back in business. Or hell, forget Doc. You know you and me can do a lot more on our own. Just like on this trip. We don't need anybody else. I've been saying it all year."

"Yes, you have." Half listening.

"Dill Schiller's doing a lot on his own. And Jack Nolan and Curley. Hell, some people call them two the Black Jack gang. They ain't got any skills we don't got."

"Can they avoid a hemp rope?"

"Shoot—I can run rings around any damn vigilance committee somebody wants to whip up."

"I hope so."

"It's easy. With the canyons and gullies and groves of trees in these parts, it'd take a month of Sundays for somebody to find me if I didn't want to be found. Probably not then. You just don't understand how slippery I can be, son. Why there was this one time . . ."

Albert went on and on, chattering away into the night, talking Slippery Jack and horse thievin' like it would go forever. Like Boots and Windy hadn't been hanged, and Doc Middleton hadn't gotten himself hitched.

Like there weren't any vigs prowling the night with sturdy hemp ropes.

Like I wasn't even there.

Chapter Fifteen

During the next week, we had no luck selling those two damn drunken-*K* horses. They followed us around northeast Nebraska, and I fed 'em whenever we stopped, shelling out payment to homesteaders or grain freighters from the money Al gave me from Otto Randolph's piebald.

I got so's I could move more or less without feeling like I had a straight-razor lodged in my rib cage or a rock in my gullet. My mouth still hurt, and I wouldn't be eating any apples for a while, but I got to imagining a gold tooth like Doc had might look pretty snappy, so I didn't worry much.

One day we parked the red dun and the grulla at the stable in Paddock and went to the café for lunch and a drink, where, lo and behold, there behind the counter was the black-bearded man who we'd tried to sell horses to right after we met the Cernek family. He tossed a mush-mouthed greeting our way as soon as we cleared the batwing doors of Humpy's Tavern.

It was one of those saloons where midday the shadows were already thick and black, and there was a shroud of smoke thick over the walls and tables and stools. The bar was a long walnut counter with wood bark still hanging for dear life on the natural side of the rough-cut board. The top was polished, had a couple place settings.

Perched on a high stool at one of the plates sat a giant of a man weighing at least two hundred fifty pounds. More than six feet tall, he unencumbered himself of a long morning coat as we walked in, tossing it over the counter. Lose the coat, he still wasn't dressed for the hot weather, wearing a wool salt and pepper suit. I wondered if maybe he had a firearm inside his suit jacket.

The man's eyes were clear and bright, his nose long and narrow. He wore a family-man's mustache on his upper lip, and his sideburns were greased up and pointed. Atop his head was a wide-brimmed flat hat like the Mormons wear, or I guess what I think of as a Mormon hat. I'm not religious; maybe Methodists wear 'em, too. The man had a steaming cup of coffee in front of him. Right away, I was suspicious of him.

Blackbeard's meaty paws slammed with a welcome.

"Howdy, boys. You still in the horse-flesh business?"

The big fellow got a kick out of it and gave us a broad smile waiting for a reply.

"Only if it's what you're making stew out of," I said, cautious. "You remember my friend and me. We're lightning-rod salesmen."

Albert asked about a drink. "You still favorin' sour mash beer—maybe selling a mug or two?"

"Best beer around. Penny a jug."

"You Humpy?"

"I've been called worse." Again, he slapped the big walnut counter. "What'll you have to eat?"

Last time we'd seen Humpy and his rock-headed friends they were playing cards in a roadhouse not far from Old Baldy, close to where the Cernek boys beat the tar out of us. I'd been less than enthusiastic about revisiting the same country but figuring Paddock was far enough west to avoid trouble. Now with this big man at the counter, I was kicking myself.

I made a quick scan of the room, my eyes adjusting to the shadows after sunlight. There didn't appear to be anybody else around. Al's walk across the hard-packed dirt floor was a strut.

He pulled out a chair at a round oak table and plopped down.

"Lightning-rod salesmen, eh?" the big man said. He had an odd accent to his talk. Sort of like a British cowboy I knew once. Or maybe from Canada. Albert lived in Canada when he was little, and he talked that same way sometimes.

"Tell me," the man said, real jovial, like he was telling a joke, but he wasn't—he was asking a question. "What would it cost to have you set up a two-story frame house with gabled roof?"

I answered him with a question of my own. "You live around these parts, mister?"

"I might." Playing it close to the vest.

"We couldn't tell you what it would cost until we saw the house."

"I'd welcome your best estimate."

"We couldn't get to the job for a while. If you're in a hurry . . ."

"No hurry."

Humpy cut through the conversation. "What are you boys eating?"

Albert piped up. "Figure we'll have steak and potatoes. Smother it with onions."

Humpy shook his head. "No steak. We done chickens yesterday."

"We'll each have a chicken then."

"Already spoken for. Got some men coming in tonight for supper."

"What do you have then?"

"Breaded gizzards and scrambled eggs. No taters."

"Fair enough."

"Two dollars a plate."

Al nearly fell out of his chair. "Are you having fun with me, Humpy?"

"It's the last of the eggs now the chickens are gone. Eggs is valuable."

My grumbling stomach was in a hurry. "How about you give us one plate and throw in a beer for each of us."

Humpy scratched his heavy black beard and pretended to do some ciphering on the countertop with his finger. "Gizzards, eggs, two beers . . . how about a dollar and ten?"

"How about a dollar," Al said.

"You twisted my arm. I'll get to warming up them gizzards."

"Bring the beer first."

Humpy disappeared into a back room behind the bar without a reply.

The big man was still half turned in our direction, waiting for me to start talkin' lightning rods again.

Dumb, dumb, dumb.

I didn't know coyote scat about no lightning rods. I should've said we was cowboys or farmers.

Before he could speak, I started in on him with a few nosey questions of my own.

"What's your name, mister? What do you do?"

He seemed to welcome the attention.

"My name's Llewellyn. William Henry Harrison . . . Lewellyn. I'm a . . . salesman of sorts myself."

"What'cha selling?"

"What do you need?" He laughed like it was the grandest joke in the world. It being such a dumb answer, I had to grin, but Al wasn't having it. He turned away from the man to look around the room.

I was more used to the dim interior now and stood up.

While Llewellyn watched, I walked around, letting my heels thump into the floor, admiring some of the junk Hump had hanging on the walls. Above a tintype photograph of a dance hall girl, he had set a pair of Mexican spurs—"Wonder where he got these?"—and in the far back corner was an upright rinky-dink piano.

"Problem with these is nobody ever knows how to play 'em. Sat in a bar in Dakota once and the damn fella played the same tune all night. Must've heard "Rose of Montana" three hundred times." I called out to the bar. "D'you play, Mr. Llewellyn?"

"It's been a long time," he said.

"Where you from, if you don't mind me asking?"

"I'm from Wisconsin. My family is Welsh. Where you from, son?"

Al jumped into the mix, joining me at the piano. "I can play 'The Chop Waltz.' You want to hear?"

"No, you can't."

"Bet lunch?"

"A dollar? Shoot."

He cracked his knuckles and bent over the keyboard with a heavy sigh. "Cut the small talk with the sheepherder, will you? I'm pretty sure he's a cop."

But he said it so only I could hear.

I gave Albert some piano instructions loud enough Llewellyn heard me. "You're supposed to put your fingers on the white keys, Sam." Calling my friend Sam was a sudden, mad inspiration just in case he was right about the big man.

"I know where to put my fingers," Al said. "I was just seeing if you knew."

He hit the first sour note.

"Sounds like Trudy's little milk calf."

"Shucks, this wooly big piece of furniture is out of tune. I can't play 'The Chop Waltz' on a piano that's out of tune."

"Pay up," I said.

"How about you play us something, Gus?"

"I got the same problem you did." I crossed the floor back to my chair and fell into it. My war wounds mostly healed, I still felt a twinge in my shoulder. "Except I'm still half crippled. Otherwise, I might play you that waltz."

Llewellyn again: "Oh, have you been recently injured?"

I winked. "Farmer's daughter. 'Bout broke my spine. You know how it is for us salesmen."

Humpy carried our drinks out from behind the bar. "Who's playing a waltz?"

"Al was going to play 'The Chop Waltz.' "

"You need to tune your piano, Hump."

Once we were both back at the table, Humpy bent over to speak intimately so's Llewellyn couldn't eavesdrop.

"I ought to tell you fellas to forgo any horse trading while you're in town."

Al took a drink from his mug and wiped the foam from his upper lip with a long sleeve.

"Oh?"

"The men I mentioned before, the ones coming in for supper? They really are coming in for supper. No joke. Three of 'em—from Lincoln. This man at the bar is one of them."

"All right."

"They work for the government. Or at least I think he does."

I felt a jolt like I'd been wired up to a string of those electric batteries I heard about. "Who are they?"

"What do they want?" said Al.

"There's a long story goes with it."

I drank half my beer and tried to sit still.

Humpy sniffed the air and pushed off toward the kitchen. "We'll talk more after I get your lunch."

Al leaned back in his chair and watched Humpy go. Then he turned slatted eyes to me. "This feels like a trap," he said. "You think these men are laying a trap for us, Gus?"

"I don't think so."

And I meant it, even though Humpy's spiel had me nervous as a sassy newborn kitten.

"If it's anything, it's these men are big business boys looking to stake some kind of claim up here. Humpy doesn't want us getting our nose in it is all."

Al sat forward and drummed his fingers on the table. His beer went untouched.

"You gonna drink your beer?"

"Something stinks," he said. "Other than the damn gizzards."

Because the oily smoke of sizzling lard and hen meat filled the room with a pungent, palpable smell.

"If you're not gonna drink your beer, I'll take it."

Humpy carried out a pot of coffee and filled Llewellyn's cup. Neither of the men paid any more attention to us.

"You're the one been talking vigilance committees," Al said. He kicked backwards in his chair. "Let's get out of here."

But it was too late. As the legs of his chair scraped the dirt, two shadows appeared on the boardwalk outside the batwings. I had only a glimpse of them as they stopped, each of them talking over the other. One had his back to me. He was the shortest, with a round derby hat and a tweed suit. The taller one in front of him was losing his hair in front but wore a trim mustache and a black gentleman's suit.

At the counter, Llewellyn noticed their presence and walked past our table toward the door. He nodded to Al and me, then joined his friends on the boardwalk. They sang like magpies at the flower garden for less than a minute, then clomped away from the door like all three of 'em were joined at the hip.

I heard one of the men say something about checking on his horse before lunch.

As quickly as they disappeared, Humpy was back at our table lugging a plate the size of the Dakota territory with a devil's tower of hot chicken meat.

"Where's the eggs?" I said.

"You'll have to dig for them."

"Get another beer? No extra charge?"

"I suppose it'll be okay."

"Bring one for my friend."

Humpy handed each of us a fork. "I don't believe you ever told me your names."

"No, we didn't," I said.

Al hooked a thumb over his shoulder. "What about Llewellyn and those other two outside?"

"Ah," Humpy said. "Let me get the fresh beer."

Al lashed out fast as a prairie rattler, snagging hold of Humpy's wrist with an iron grip. "You tell us now, mister." The tone in his voice left the bearded barkeep no choice.

He yanked his arm free but pulled out a third chair and fell down into it. "Fair enough," he said. "But you'll get a blasted earful."

We waited as Humpy rubbed his wrist.

"Eat, eat." He urged us toward our forks. "It's not the kind of news you want on an empty stomach."

I picked up my fork and mined down through the greasy gizzards to where the cooked egg yolks were buried. What I brought up was cold and had a light brown film coating but tasted better than what I'd grown up on. "Start talking," I said.

"You ever heard of Colonel Jim O'Beirne?" He pronounced it *Beer-knee*.

"Nope."

"Jim's my brother-in-law, an Indian agent up to Pine Ridge."

"Married to your sister, is he?" Humpy's fat fingers wore no rings.

"Matter of fact. She's a peach."

"Get on with it," Albert said through a mouth loaded with

meat. He gave me the hairy eyeball, and Humpy pushed on.

"Earlier this year, Jim got a whiney letter from Chief Little Wound, bitching about how his horses are being stole. And when they ain't bein' stole, they're bein' traded off for a single bottle of whiskey. So Jim's been shouldering Little Wound's burden for a while already anyway, but this letter was especially mean spirited."

"Mean spirited how?"

"Like Little Wound's ready-to-go-on-the-warpath-and-burn-some-shit-down mean spirited."

"What did Jim do?"

"Only thing he could do was talk to Governor Nance. Well, it just so happens Nance is already jawin' with some ranchers about their own missing horses."

Al waved away the news like it was a pesky house fly. "I'll bet I can guess who. Some of these crybaby cowboys got no more balls than Queen Victoria."

"Apparently he's been talking to a good many old fellas. These men are from our area right hereabouts."

Al chuckled between bites and gulped his beer. "How many? Three or four?"

"Three hundred."

I coughed without covering my mouth, and a wad of chewed gristle hit the table, then bounced to the floor. "Three . . . hundred?"

"Like I say, it ain't news for an empty stomach. But there's more."

Al sat frozen in place. "Say it."

"The wealthiest ten men put up a thousand dollars each to bring in Doc Middleton."

Al let out a big breath of air, and I pushed away my plate.

Before either of us could reply, Humpy gave each of us a quick nod. "I know, boys. I know. It's a damn shame. Doc's a good man." He glanced down at Al's holster.

" 'Fraid we might kill the messenger, Hump?"

"What's all this have to do with the three men here in Paddock?"

"I heard from McFarlane over at the livery these men are special agents up from the governor's office, snooping around. Trafficking in stolen Indian horses and trading whiskey with 'em . . . well, it's a federal offense. Then there's the local thievery. The homesteaders don't feel safe. The Indians are all riled up. It makes for an untenable situation."

You could tell he liked using the word *untenable*. Made him feel smart.

Al tossed down his fork. "Detectives, huh?"

"Just so."

"I ain't got much use for detectives," he said. "I think it's time to ride on out."

"I haven't finished my eggs," I said.

"You're finished. Let's go."

"Hold on—three shakes."

Humpy said, "Let's call it a dollar."

"Let's call it on the house, and you're lucky I don't cave in your skull. I thought you knew us."

Humpy's face went red, but he kept his temper bottled up tight. "I know you," he said. "Why do you think I was telling you all this about those men going after Doc?"

"If you know who we are, then you know we're good for a meal or a beer whenever we step inside this rotten place." Al turned to me again. "Let's us get."

I had a mouthful of eggs and was swirling the remains of my beer at the bottom of my mug. "Them three were headed over to the horse barn a minute ago. We walk over to saddle up, we're liable to run into them. We're better off waiting here."

"Do you think those other two men know you?"

"Not by sight," I said. "Depends who they are."

I put a lot of gravel into my voice for Humpy. "Besides Mr. William-Mary-what's-his-name Llewellyn, do you know 'em? Have they given you their names?"

Humpy shook his head. "I don't know 'em, but Llewellyn said their names. One of them is Hazen."

"Hmmm. Not familiar to me," I said, looking at Al shake his head. He didn't know Hazen either.

Humpy said, "The third man is a round-faced little *Dutchman.* Not sure of his name, but he sure seems to know Doc."

I stifled the urge to cough again.

"This . . . uh, little Dutchman. He wouldn't, by chance, be an agent of the Wyoming Stock Grower's Association?"

"Yes, sir. I'm sure he is." Humpy snapped his fingers as it came to him. "Lykins. His name is Billy Lykins."

Oh, boy.

"Shit, shit, shit. We gotta go." I stood up, immediately disoriented. "Back door?"

"There's a back door out of the kitchen."

As if at the cue of some heavenly stage manager, I heard the thud of boots on the boardwalk outside. Enter Lykins, Llewellyn, and their friend.

I clamped my hat down hard over my eyes and walked as fast as I could toward the kitchen with Albert in tow.

"Boys . . . wait." But Humpy's attention was divided as the three men stepped over the threshold, Lykins removing his domed bowler. "Do you have a spot of lunch, barkeep?"

Al was fast on my heels as I tore through the kitchen and hit the outside door.

Bam! Open. *Slam,* shut.

"Hurry up, hurry up," I said.

"What's lit fire under you so fast?"

"Lykins is in there. It's Billy Lykins."

"I caught as much. So why the panic?"

"You don't understand. Tell you later."

Practically tripping over my boots, I managed to find my horse and climb in the saddle. Albert paid off the stable manager and followed behind.

We hightailed it out of the country pretty damn fast.

Who could have imagined the one man we'd cross paths with was a man ruthlessly determined to bring all us Pony Boys to justice? A man feverish and gleeful in the pursuit, a sick bastard who found joy in tracking men down and executing them.

Who could have imagined it would be Billy Lykins, a man I'd met before face to face?

A man who could've immediately recognized me.

Chapter Sixteen

We rode onto Henry Richardson's claim and parked our horses, along with the red dun and black-tailed grulla, behind the pole barn where I had seen all the women of the wedding party smiling and laughing and smoking cigarettes two weeks before. I was lonely for Trudy and feeling odd and out of my body like I had when we first pulled into Pleasant Valley.

The truth is, I was worn out from the trail. The notion of Billy Lykins pointing me out as a horse thief to Llewellyn and Hazen had my guts in knots.

The day had gone from sunny to gray, like a canvas tarp was tossed over the sky, cutting off the light, but also dry like winter potato sacks.

On the way from Paddock, Al told me Doc Middleton and Pood were supposed to be settling down near Atkinson, but nobody knew exactly where, which was natural enough because Doc never stayed in one place for long. Everybody's heard the old saying about a man not letting grass grow under his feet. "He could be anyplace by now," I said.

Wherever Doc was, he wasn't at the scene of his wedding, and with those stock detectives after him, I hoped he was as far away as he could get. Maybe back in Texas. Or California.

Just thinking about Llewellyn sitting there at the bar, all pie and whipped cream and sweetie smiles, made my skin crawl.

Al had asked questions on the trail, and I told him.

"You said Lykins might recognize you? How's it possible? I

never heard of you two crossing paths."

"It was back in '77 when I first rode with Doc. Lykins was working for the Wyoming cattlemen, and there was a sheriff out there gunning for us. He was a rough bird, but likable. Everybody liked his sense of humor. He was a fun-loving man, but dead serious like a willow-switched coonhound on the hunt. Well, he had so many friends, getting a posse up was easy enough for him, and Lykins joined his force."

I hadn't told anybody about those early years with Doc, and it broke me up to tell Al, him all sober and upset because of Humpy's. We were both hungry is all.

It's the kind of story ought to be told around a campfire.

"But anyway," I said, "this posse of men had us cornered out by the Kansas border, and Lykins, the crazy little Dutchman, just charges in at me and Doc and the others, guns a-blazing. Pepper Scoots and Chet Tanner was with us then."

I could tell Al wanted me to get to the point.

"Lykins comes in on me first, and I'll never forget—seeing me tripped him up. 'You're just a kid,' he says to me. He shouldn't have paused in his charge, because it gave Doc time to get a bead on him with a rifle. Lykins would be feeding the worms right now if it weren't for Doc's pulling the trigger, and . . . nothing! I'll be a speckled hen, but Doc's rifle jammed at the last minute."

"You and Doc went to jail, didn't you?"

"No, sirree—I did not. After Doc's gun let him down, Lykins went after him hard. In the middle of the dust-up, I scooted away down a little crick bed and got clean away. But yeah—Lykins got Doc, which was why he was shacked up in Sidney for a while. Not so long—he had some help and got away."

"But you say Lykins got a good look at you. Dammit, Gus—bad luck."

"It was a few years ago, sure, but I don't want to take a

chance on him recognizing me."

"Bad luck about the rifle not firing."

"It was one of those things sometimes happens. A million to one, but nothing can be done about it. Everything turned out okay," I said.

"But Lykins is out there again now. Damn."

Al seemed especially bothered now, and we didn't trade another word until landing at the ranch.

Henry Richardson's place was cold and lonesome as a tomb. I made a special point of not looking at the woodshed where I'd lost face with Trudy—more, with myself.

I wished I could meet up with Curley Grimes again sometime, maybe get the drop on him with my thundering pistol.

Squeaky, I never wanted to see her again.

Albert hallooed the house, and I called out for young Ted.

"Ted Roberts! Hey, Ted. It's Albert Wade and Gus. Come on out, pard."

No answer but for a black and yellow-winged grasshopper, dusky-brown grasshopper against the emerald grass. Springing to life, he leapt into a mad flight. Was a time, not so long ago I thought, when I would've chased the grasshopper across the lawn, diving to catch him between cupped hands between hops, becoming a grasshopper myself, or a hungry red-tailed hawk swooping down to gorge myself on the fat 'baccy-chewing bug.

Now as I kicked through the grass up the sweeping incline to the house, the grasshopper bored me.

"Any luck?"

"Nope," Al said.

The Haptonstall house was empty. The Richardson family appeared to be gone.

"Where'd everybody go?" I said, doing my best to ignore the goosepimples rising on my arm. Shucks, it was barely getting on to dusk, and the afternoon heat still came off the earth in waves.

The house was still so run down, just like it was the last time we were here, but now I noticed the foundation was crumbling into the sod, like a great steamship listing in the muddy river, threatening to capsize. The breeze felt clammy, and a strange tan moth kept flitting past my face.

The entire scene was crawling into my imagination like a bad dream, and I jumped at every bird sound or creak of a door hinge. Again, I said, "Where is everybody?"

Al picked up the tremor in my voice and taunted me. "Gone to the booses?"

Trudy's spirits of dead children.

I knew of at least three kids drowned in the Niobrara on the other side of the place, and in my loco state of mind, I imagined them inside the house, waiting for somebody to follow home.

"You shut your pie hole," I said. I wasn't kidding. I was ready to box his ears. I'd had enough of Kid Wade and his smart-ass mouth on this trip.

Al climbed onto the front porch and pushed his way into the house. "I guess nobody would mind if we helped ourselves to some grub."

Fearing I'd pick up a haunting, I decided to stay outside.

Cupping my hands around my mouth, I called out again. "Ted Roberts? Henry?"

Albert tromped back outside with an armload of bread, a package of bacon, and a wax paper sack I later discovered was full of oatmeal cookies. Wafting out through the door came the stuffy smell of enclosed spaces. With the recent days' heat, no way they'd have kept the windows shut up such a way. It had been a few days since anybody was home.

Al's words echoed my thoughts. "They haven't been here for a while. Be a service to 'em if we go ahead and eat this pork meat 'fore it goes bad."

He was right, of course, but I was still wary of the place and not sure I wanted to eat. I'd made two days' ride on coffee and a few forkfuls of Humpy's gizzards and eggs. Never had I been so hungry but so queasy at the same time.

All I could think about was Trudy.

"Let's move on home to Pleasant Valley."

"Not until after we eat," Al said. "I'm nothing but bones. Let's go down to where they cooked the pig at Doc's wedding. We can put up some wood and start a fire."

I wanted to argue with Al, but then I saw Ted walking out from the barn. He wore his glasses strapped to his face and a tall Stetson as big around as his waist. I think the spectacles kept his hat from covering his head like a knight's iron helmet. And his big wide ears.

He stopped close to our horses and gave them a long, appraising look.

I hollered out. "Ted! Ted Roberts."

He turned at my voice and lifted his arm to wave.

"At least somebody's home," I said.

"I'm bringing the food anyway."

I felt better meeting Ted under the roof of the open pole barn, like the boy's presence scared the booses back under the river water. Albert put his stolen groceries on a rough-hewn picnic table, and now I thought maybe a bite of salt pork would hit the button.

"What are you fellows doing here?" Ted said. He squawked like a goose, or one of those parrots in the gypsy carnivals. If he was glad to see us, he didn't show it. Actually, he seemed fairly annoyed with our visit. Like maybe we'd been sent to check up on him. Al lit into him like he was the sheriff of all Nebraska.

"Been yelling for you close to an hour, where the hell is everybody, Ted?"

"I was sleeping."

"Why aren't you up to the house?"

"Too hot. Windows are all painted shut." He fingered his glasses and fiddled with his hat. Ted was always chewing his nails or biting the skin off his calluses or bothering his face with a scratch. "I been staying out here in the barn 'cause it's cooler."

I looked into the open front of the three-walled place, back to where the ground met up with the back timbers. Ted had a pile of straw there, and I could see an old lantern and some leather war bags.

He was playing Indian camp-out in his own backyard.

"Best don't go starting a fire with your lantern." I couldn't help but give Ted some advice, him being younger than me. "Liable to catch the straw with a spark and—whoosh!"

"Don't go lecturing me, August John. I been cooking beans and coffee and chocolate on the little stove over there."

"You've got chocolate?"

"Not anymore." He was proud to say it.

The little stove he pointed at was the same big iron grill I'd seen them roast a pig on. The night Doc tied the knot it had been a blazing thing alive with fire and hickory smoke. Now it sat cold and black.

Al decided to light it. He piled some grass under the grill. From inside his pants pocket he pulled a match, struck it on his rough leather holster, and caught the little nest on fire. Spindly wisps of smoke curled around. "Get some more kindling, hey, Ted?"

Ted and I both gathered enough rough, dry chaff for a fire, and before long we had enough flame to fry the bacon in a pan. Al used a fork to stir the meat around as it popped and snapped.

While we waited, I tucked eagerly into the sack of cookies.

Wouldn't you know the dough was full of raisins.

But being half starved from our time on the trail, I chewed 'em up and swallowed anyway. I decided it was rude to eat all of Ted's cookies, so I tilted the sack to him, offering some.

"You can have 'em," Ted said. "I don't like raisins. She puts 'em in there because she likes 'em. Makes more for her, see?"

"Where's your parents?" I said, around a mouthful of oatmeal.

"Out of this damn country. Someplace safe. Where you two should be."

"Why ain't you with 'em?"

"I stayed to watch the cows." Again the sense of pride. In fact, Ted Roberts might've been the damndest proud little tenderfoot I ever did see. For such a little pissant, he got along well enough, but I didn't appreciate his unsolicited advice.

Ted was half a foot shorter than me, and light as a blade of bluestem. I plucked him from his position and steered him over to the table beside Al, where I set him down, harder than maybe I should have. "You better explain yourself, Ted. What makes you think you can tell us what to do or where to go?"

Ted's eyeballs were magnified by his glasses, and they rolled when they moved from one side of his head to the other. He looked at Albert for help. Then back to me. Then to Albert.

Finally, just to change the subject, he took a shine to my gun and peppered me with questions.

"You're carrying a Colt? Six shooter, right? Single action or double action or what? I wish'd I could maybe shoot it. Would you let me shoot it, Gus? I'm a crack shot, I am. You just ask anybody. Ask Pood, or anybody." I thought I was gonna croak listening to the little turd and almost gave him a swat across the chops.

Al smacked him on the back of the head, knocking his hat sideways. "Shut up, Ted."

I said, "You've got a secret to tell, so spill it."

Ted started in squawking again. "You don't have to go whipping me."

The bacon crisped and the fire crackled and Ted chewed his fingers.

"Just say what's going on here," I said. "We've been out Paddock way, and farther. Where do you think we got them two horses?"

Along with our guns, Ted had been eyeing the horses since we started talking to him. At first, when I saw him standing in the middle of the ranch yard alone, I felt sorry he'd drank Ol' Bowlegs mix and got sick. Now I wished we had some to force down his gullet.

I rolled up my fingers and pushed the fist up under his nose. "Spill it."

Al got busy pulling fried bacon out of the pan and laying it out on the wood table to cool. It smelled delicious.

Ted swallowed hard and started to talk.

"Some men showed up night before last," Ted said. "They were wearing dark masks over all their faces with holes cut out so they could see."

"How many men were there?"

"Three. They rode a trio of sassy black mares, and one of them, I think he was the leader man, he had a long cape covering his shirt, so I couldn't tell who he was. I didn't know who any of them were. Ma said for me to get lost down to the barn or wherever. So I hid out like a bandit."

"Why were they at your house, Ted? What was it they wanted?"

"The head man said they was from the vigilance committee. Said they were looking for Jack Nolan and Curley Grimes on account of Nolan stole so and so's horse, and maybe one or two other pony boys were in on it, but I didn't hear who."

The story hit me like a sack of flour in the guts. First Llewellyn and his government detectives. Now an honest-to-Betsy vigilance committee—and they were looking for us.

I started putting the jigsaw puzzle together. I had always been slow to start problem solving, but, once I had the basic outline, things made sense to me pretty fast.

"Al, these must be the stinkin' devils who killed Boots and Windy."

"They weren't looking for Doc?" Al said.

"Ah-yuh, they was." And Ted's voice got crazy then, high spirited and fast like the rinky-dink piano in the Paddock saloon except the strings were stretched to breaking and squeaked and pinged in between his words. Like maybe he was going to be sick or suddenly grow up right in front of our eyes—I wasn't sure which way he was going to go.

In the end, he didn't do either one. He was just this dumb kid who watched his family get sweated by vigs.

"They badgered Henry, saying where's Doc, and where's Curley Grimes, and we got to hang those skunks before that bastard in Lincoln pardons them."

It was the first time I heard about a pardon, so I pushed him. "What pardon are you talking about? You gotta remember something more, Ted."

"They said Nance, the governor's name. He's third governor now—one of the men said. Ain't it something Nebraska's had three governors?"

"Who cares?"

"Henry said later when they said *Nance,* they meant the governor. But Henry didn't know from no pardon, neither. Henry said the hooded men were saying all kinds of nonsense just to confuse us."

"Henry is a good man, Ted," Al said. "He wouldn't give nobody up."

"Henry ain't seen nobody since Doc's wedding night. It's the truth, and he stuck to it. But once the men rode off, he figured to get the hell out and lay low for a spell—just in case they come back."

"Surprised they left you here."

"The riders never saw me."

"A kid alone. You sure you can handle it?"

"Somebody's got to stay and watch the animals."

He meant it. I had to give it to him, Ted was tougher than he looked. The spectacles made him seem weak, and the way he generally moped around, acting like he had a cob in his butt, didn't help him.

Some people walk different than others. It doesn't mean anything about what's inside.

Al patted the kid on the shoulder, sauntered around the front of the barn, pacing back and forth while he crunched down on his bacon pieces. I saw him eye a pair of milking cows in the nearby corral. "How much livestock you got around here, Ted?"

The boy ignored the question. "You don't mind me saying so, Albert, you two ought to go on now. Go back where you came from. Those vigilance men had guns. Who knows when they will come back?"

"What kinds of guns did they have?" I said.

"Long rifles. Carbines. Two of them had guns at the hip. Like you do."

Al wasn't to be deterred. "The livestock, Ted?"

Ted shook his head and stood up as tall as possible.

"A dozen, not counting the chickens or my own horse. Got ten head of cattle down below the water gap. Them two there are for milking, but one's about to calf." While we watched, Al paced over to the corral and opened the gate.

The black Angus cows reminded me of Betty, and I got a sense we needed to hurry then, get on to Pleasant Valley. I was worried about the vigilantes paying Trudy a visit, and I was battle sore and weary from our rough adventures. I had to bite my bacon with the side of my mouth, and my ribs were still tender.

Al knew I was antsy, but his attention was firmly on the cows.

"How about we put those two horses we brung from out east into the pen with your cows. They'll get along well enough, ya think?"

"I don't think you ought to do it, Albert." I didn't want Ted to end up like Boots and Windy if the vigs came back and found stolen horses in with the cows.

"I'm thinking if these men are on the prowl like you say, we ought not be seen with any extra horses. You can see how it makes sense?"

"I can see it," said Ted, but he wasn't quite sure.

I wasn't sure either, not after all the time and money I'd shelled out shepherding those two drunken-*K* louses hither and yon across the whole sorry country. But I could see Al had a gleam in his eye, and I knew he wouldn't budge until he got his way.

This was more and more typical of the way things were playing out.

Al lifted a coil of rope off one of the corral fence posts. "Here, Ted, you lead these two cows out and put them someplace else, if it makes you more comfortable. I want those two horses in this pen. You want to go get them for us, Gus?"

I couldn't see what difference it made where the horses were. If we were going to leave them behind, Ted could find a place to shack 'em up, but then I figured maybe Albert was trying to help the kid out some before we left. He had a good point about not being seen on the road.

When I brought up the grulla and the dun and put 'em in the pen, Ted and Al each led out a cow.

"Close the gate, Gus."

I did as Al ordered. When the three of us were standing there in the near darkness with two cows and fireflies sparking up the air, tracing green whorls in space, Albert said I should go get our saddle nags. "Hurry up, Gus, we ain't got all night."

I hustled down the hill, but the horses weren't where we'd left them. I wasn't sure which way to turn. Pretty soon, here comes Ted leading the critters to me like he was born to drovering. "Where's your cow?" I said, otherwise dumbstruck.

He said, "I put her down behind the woodshed." I still didn't want to think about the woodshed.

"No moon tonight. A good night for travel," he said.

It's true, and Al had mentioned it the night before when the last sliver of the waning crescent was like a glowing fingernail scratching at the bejeweled ceiling above.

Without light a man can travel unseen.

But Ted wasn't done pitching advice. Back up top of the hill, the kid told me and Al, "You watch out for the lamplight on Lantern Hill." He hissed it out like he was almost too scared to mention it. Like Lantern Hill was a dirty word or devil's oath, something to get him cast into the pit or spanked by his ma. Neither one of us knew what he meant.

I said, "Where's Lantern Hill?"

He said it was what the vigilance committee called the tall steeple of rock on the north bank of the Niobrara when you followed the Black Hills trail. The top of the butte was like a damn mountain, taller'n Old Baldy. You could see it from a million miles away. "When the lantern shines, the vigilantes ride," he said, almost like it was a memorized part of a poem.

I said, "Is that what they told you?"

"It's what they told Henry and be damned if you can't see it from here. Right after they left, we looked for it and could just make it out."

For once, my directions were screwed silly. I tried to imagine in my head where Lantern Hill was in relation to where I stood on Richardson's place.

"Yonder past the stand of cottonwoods on the horizon," Ted said. I squinted my lids, peering hard at the deep indigo mantle floating on a sea of black rock.

I imagined a brief flash. But it was only a firefly.

"I don't see a durn thing," Al said. It was the kind of spooky goings-on he despised.

I threw myself onto the chestnut, light and easy, and whispered praise in her ear. "We gotta hurry now, gal." But Al was moseying around with the milk cow like a Pony Express rider who'd clocked in his segment of the trail and now had all the time in the world. Or maybe a homesteader trailing in with his faithful old cow.

Eventually, he collected up what was left of the cookies, tossing me a sack of crumbs. "We'll polish those off later."

Then Al handed me the lead on the milk cow while he crawled onto his horse.

"You keep your eye out for that lamplight, Ted."

"Where you going with my cow, Albert?"

Al held out his hand, and I transferred the hemp string back over to him. "We'll keep her safe and milked every morning. Count on it."

"You can't just walk out of here with my cow."

"Lookee over there in the pen, Ted. You got two fine horses in trade."

"Who owns the drunken-*K*? You ain't no drunken-*K*. We all three know where them horses came from."

"Oh?" Al said. "Suppose you tell me?"

"Drunken-*K* is Herko Koster's brand over to Knox County."

Across the space between our horses, I kicked Al in the shin. "Thought you said *K* was for Clausen?"

"Did I say such a thing?"

"You did."

Al looked at me like I had three heads. "Gus, Clausen begins with the letter *C*."

"I've never heard of Herko Koster," I said.

"Nobody has," Al said. He tipped his hat back to Ted. "I appreciate the trade."

"You can't walk away with my cow."

Ted didn't understand.

Al couldn't help it. Thievin' was in his blood.

Ted continued to hoot and call and jump up and down, but he didn't stand in our way as we rode away from the ranch. We followed a roundabout path through a hedgerow of cedars, then down through the grass into a ravine until we came to a long, tall hill of grazed fescue. The slope presented itself against the stars, gradual and smooth, and we took to climbing.

With no moon, the sky was awash with speckled beauty.

After a while, I thought to ask about Richardson's cow.

"You don't think it's a fair trade? We need something in trade for those drunken-*K* horses."

With a vigilance committee on the loose, the wise move was to leave them behind.

I didn't pester him anymore, but he continued to talk like I was. "If you gotta know everything, I'll tell you the truth. This cow is my new present for Trudy."

"She's already got a cow."

"Nobody can have too many cows."

"I know it's just—"

"Tch." Albert held up his hand, pressing his horse in the ribs. "Stand still. Hold up a second."

He stretched out his arm, and the wind blew across our hilltop perch with a renewed sense of urgency. If the booses made me shiver before, now they had my back teeth chattering.

There, far off in the distance on Lantern Hill, a light was burning.

Chapter Seventeen

It was just like Trudy to act like our comings and goings were natural as ducks flying south for the winter, and when we rode in long after midnight, she didn't utter a peep. Moses McGee woke her up with a barking to lift Lazarus, and, when she came outside, Al presented her with Richardson's cow. She took it to the barn without comment.

"She's half asleep, poor dear," Al said. "You wait until morning. She'll be loving all over me because of her new cow." I waited for Trudy to come out of the barn, and, when she did, I tried to get between her and the front door. She couldn't give a fig about me. She brushed past like I was untouchable as the night sky.

I didn't blame her.

After the spectacle I'd made of myself with Squeaky and then disappearing for more than two weeks, Trudy must've felt pretty done wrong. And lonesome. Sure, she saw Sonny Clausen, who came almost every Tuesday, and maybe homesteaders like Otto Randolph and his wife, a few other freighters now and again. But most days it was Trudy, all by herself, talking to Betty and Buddy. And they weren't much for visiting.

Plus I knew she was full of sorrow living by herself with her memories of Al's stepdad and now me, and how I'd gone and betrayed her . . . for what?

I'd spent every last cent of the money Al gave me for Randolph's piebald, and neither of us had seen a damn dime from the Pine Ridge horses. Not for the first time, I wondered what this life of foolishness was earning me.

I bedded down in the straw across from Betty's pen. Al was already down and snoring.

Then next morning Buddy started bleating before sunup, and I dutifully crawled into the stall with Betty to help him eat. Incredible how much he'd grown in two weeks—and a testament to Trudy's good care.

The cow acted like she didn't know me. When Betty shook her head and groused, I said, "Easy now, girl," but she charged me.

I jumped up to the side of the stall and, falling over, flopped to the ground like such a greenhorn, I'm embarrassed to tell about it. Al was already gone to the house so at least I didn't lose face in front of him. Some cowman I was. Here I was thinking of settling down in Pleasant Valley.

I tossed my shirt on overtop my trousers and walked outside barefoot.

Al was there at the door, already saddled up.

I hadn't noticed his horse was missing, but here he was fixing to ride out, and I was still half asleep. He chewed a stem of grass as he tossed a thumb back in the direction of the house.

"Trudy won't talk to me. Like I did something to hurt her feelings."

"Did you get some breakfast?"

"No."

"Not a cup of coffee?"

"Says we can both drop dead far as she's concerned."

I chewed my bottom lip. "You wait. I'll go talk to her."

"Hell with her. After I busted my ass to bring her Heavy Frahm's couch. After I give her a brand new cow."

I reminded him we never got the couch off Frahm's homestead.

He said, "Mount up, and we'll move on to Atkinson. Let's see what Doc's got brewing."

"No, no. Just give me a few minutes."

I knew Trudy wouldn't be happy with us, but she wouldn't toss us away like so much hog slop.

Drop dead? We meant more to her.

I thought *I* did.

Jamming my feet into my boots and tucking in my shirt, I spit-combed my hair, smoothing out the rooster tails. I rubbed my cheeks, realized I needed a shave.

It would have to wait.

I hurried outside, only to find Albert still sitting high in his Mex saddle. I said, "Ain't you gonna give her a second chance? What with you bringing her the new cow and all?"

Al looked out over the poll of his horse, across the valley. When he spoke, he pulled the blade of grass from his mouth.

"You know what, Gus? At this point, I'm not giving anybody a second chance. Except for maybe you."

"You know how Trudy is." I tried to explain. She needed a chance to be mad in front of us. "We'll be through the worst of it by lunchtime. Tonight will be like old times."

"I'm sick of old times. I'm ready to make some new memories."

"I've got to talk with her."

"I'm giving you a chance to ride with me, Gus."

He used an odd tone of voice, and his gaze was more intense than usual. I shrugged him off.

"If it's the same to you, I'll stay here for now." I put my hand behind my back, tried to stretch away sore muscles. "I'll catch up with you sometime."

"We all do what we have to do. I'd hate to be quits with you, Gus."

He said it like it was already half done.

"Shucks, Albert, you and me . . . why, we're not ever quits. You know it."

"I hope so."

"You talk to Doc, tell him what we found out in Paddock. About them detectives. And what Ted said about a pardon."

"He like to already knows."

Then Al spurred his mare away from the place, out across the range in a wide arc toward the scrubby tree line. For a second, I thought he was making a long circle and would come back.

But he didn't.

So I turned around, walked to the front of the house, and knocked gently.

"It's me," I said, and the door opened.

"More coffee?" I said, pouring her tin cup full to the brim.

"Thanks."

I put the pot down quiet, so as not to jar the tension still hanging in the air, and rejoined Trudy at the table. All the birds' nests and clouds of confusion from early morning were getting swept out of my head. We'd shared sour-milk pancakes, scrambled eggs, and sausage in near silence. Now only my empty plate, a cup of lukewarm coffee, and all the unsaid words remained. But just being around her, I felt more content than I had been at any time during the past couple weeks. In some ways, it scared me more than the booses.

Trudy cleared her throat. "How long you fixin' to stay this time?"

Since I'd been thinking the same thing, I had an answer all planned. "Figured I'd stay as long as you'd have me."

She nodded to herself. Like weighing my answer on a scale inside her head. She was taking stock, ciphering things out. When she opened her mouth, she took me by surprise. I thought I knew her so well. It would take me another forty years, and maybe not even now can I say I know her for sure.

"Do you mean some kind of proposal?" she said.

"Proposal for what?"

"For you staying here *proper.*"

"Ah. I see." She was talking about a wedding.

"So answer the question."

Now it was my turn to do some figuring. "As to whether or not what I said was a proposal, I guess you'd say it all depends."

"What's it all depend on?" She was getting her back up.

But I had to take the chance.

"There's a few things you have to know, and I have to know you believe them. First of all, at Doc's wedding, the girl in the woodshed . . . and me . . . we . . ."

"She's a whore, Gus. I don't know how I could be more ashamed of you than I was when I saw you with her."

"Nothing happened."

"Oh, something was happening all right."

This didn't seem to be the best road to go down.

I looked for a fork in the trail. Rather than talk about Squeaky any more, I decided to plot out my future on the table in front of her. "I think I'm done riding with Doc."

"You think? Convenient to say it, since he's all married off. What about Albert?"

"I think I'm done riding with Albert. For now."

"For now?"

"For as long as you want."

"We're back to where we started, aren't we? You still ain't said if what you're saying is a proposal."

"—"

Her eyebrows came down hard. "You need to think about what kind of man you want to be, Gus."

"I hear what you're saying. The thing is, I—"

Came a hard rap at the door, and I didn't get to finish my sentence.

Trudy stood up and smoothed out her dress.

"Are you expecting somebody?" I said.

She didn't answer. Instead, she walked to the entrance with confidence and cracked it open. When she saw who it was on the other side, she pulled the door back with a pleasant greeting. "Oh, Mr. Randolph. How good to see you."

Otto Randolph clomped in with tall black riding boots, square at the toe, his pants tucked in at the top. He gave me a genial nod, calling me by name. "Gus."

His familiarity jarred me. I nodded back.

Trudy was all professional smiles. She moved behind her store counter. "What can I do for you, sir?"

Randolph lifted his elbow, scratched the back of his neck. "Ain't so much what you can do for me, maybe what I can do for you." Then a light shone in his eye, and he remarked, "I would enjoy a cup of that coffee you make."

"Right away," Trudy said.

"You-all add eggshells to the grounds, don't you?" Randolph watched Trudy retrieve the pot and a fresh tin cup. "Been telling the wife we ought to do the same, but she keeps forgetting."

Trudy poured a cup. Handed it to him over the counter. "Eggshells smooth out the bitter."

Randolph put his finger through the cup handle and used his other hand to toss a couple pennies on the counter.

Trudy pushed the money back toward him. "No charge for coffee."

"No, ma'am. I won't be beholdin' to you." He sipped slowly, cleaning the remnants away from his mustache with a thumb.

Finally, Trudy said, "You were saying something, Mr. Randolph?"

The rancher's expression was calm but unsure as he nodded.

"I been rehearsing this all the way over here. I still ain't sure how to say it." When he looked up, his face was full of contrition. In a lot of ways, it was the same sorry, sad look Humpy shared with me and Al when he warned us about the stock detectives.

Turns out, for the same reason.

"You folks ought to know times are changing on the Niobrara. Things out here are still unorganized, but not for long." Randolph sipped his coffee.

Of course he was right. Holt County had been put together last year with O'Neill City as the county seat. It was only a matter of time until the territories west would be platted out and official governments installed.

We all knew it, but some people were more excited about the future than others.

Randolph said, "Not everybody's so welcoming of civilization."

He was looking at me, but I pressed him anyway. If the sorry son of a bitch was gonna play coy, I'd show him I wasn't going to go along with it. "Who do you mean by 'not everybody'?"

"I mean your friends. Albert Wade. Doc Middleton."

I guess he wasn't so coy after all. He plowed right on before I could answer.

"Gus, you know Middleton is wanted for killing the soldier boy out in Sidney. Self-defense or not, he's got to come before a judge."

I waited for him to get to the point.

"It turns out some of the ranchers have put up a new reward for Doc. For some of the men who ride for him, also. What you might not know is there's another set of men who want to pardon him."

Here was talk of a pardon again. "I'm interested in hearing more about it," I said.

"William Henry Harrison Llewellyn was commissioned in May as a special agent of the Department of Justice. His friend, Mr. Hazen, knows Doc. What you might not know about Hazen is he's stepbrother to "Quickshot" Scott Davis, captain of the shotgun guards on the Deadwood Stage."

I shrugged. "Don's see how's any of it matters."

"I just wanted you to know I'm not talking about amateurs."

"All right."

"What do Llewellyn and Hazen have to do with us, Mr. Randolph?" Trudy said.

"Those two have hooked up with an old boy named Lykins. Billy Lykins. You heard of him, I'll bet?"

I nodded slow.

Randolph said more for Trudy's benefit. "Lykins is a little Dutchman. Stockgrowers Association detective. These three men have been authorized to offer Middleton a pardon from Governor Nance and the United States of America in exchange for his help as a detective."

The announcement hit me like a hammer. Doc, a detective?

"What kind of detective?"

Randolph squirmed like spiders were crawling down his neck. It wasn't the last time I'd see him react in such a way.

"All this horse thievin' has got to stop. Middleton knows who and what's behind most of it. If he's willing to help, there's a clean slate in the organized territories for him."

I didn't believe it for a minute. The whole thing was a lie. If not slung together by Randolph, it was horse apples pitched by Llewellyn and Lykins.

"Doc would laugh in your face."

"Don't be so sure, boy."

"Don't call me boy, Mr. Randolph."

"Beg pardon."

I guess when pushed, he backed down easy enough.

"My question is, why did you figure on a special trip over here to tell us?" I asked.

Randolph wrinkled his forehead. Knitting his brows together, he took a hearty gulp from his cup and shook his head. "I only came over for a cup of coffee."

The next thing out of my mouth surprised me.

"You ever heard of Lantern Hill? Know what it means when the lamp shines at night?"

The rancher put his cup down on the counter. "Can't say I do."

"You maybe ought to ask Mr. Llewellyn."

Randolph held his empty hands out in front of his waist and spread his fingers wide. "If I gave you reason to believe I know these three government men personally, I apologize. I've never met any of them."

"You know an awful lot about the show for somebody never met the major players."

Randolph's scoffing laugh seemed genuine enough. "You ought to know gossip flies like the buzzards along the river. All I know is what I heard in Niobrara City during the weekend. Thought I'd share it with you is all."

He finished his coffee and walked to the door without picking up his pennies.

"If you see Middleton, you might share the news with him."

"If this story's as widespread as you say, he likely already knows."

Randolph thumbed his upper lip again. "I 'spect you're right." Then, off the cuff, "You might watch your own back. Make sure you're on the straight and narrow."

"What makes you think I'm not?"

"If you don't mind me saying so, you look a little bruised up here and there. Like maybe you've been in a tussle or two during the last couple weeks."

"I don't have any idea what you mean."

"Fair enough." He turned away like he carried a heavy weight on his shoulders. "You-all take care."

After he left, I stood up as if to make my way back to the coffeepot. Almost immediately Trudy came close, wrapping her arms around me.

I responded in kind, and she buried her face in my shirt. I didn't realize she was crying until she pulled back and looked into my face with some kind of expectation.

I didn't know what to say, so I rubbed a tear away from her cheek and kissed her forehead.

"There's nothing to cry about, honey. Everything will be fine."

"I don't think so, Gus. I don't think anything will be fine again. It's all going straight to hell."

"I'm telling you. This all might be good news for Doc. Maybe for all of us."

"Do you believe it?"

"No . . . no, not really. But I don't think it's anything to worry about." She wasn't having it. Instead, she buried her face again and started to sob.

I held her tight and after a while gently pulled back.

I cupped her chin in my hand. "What's got you so worked up?"

"Wh-what R-randolph said. Couldn't you hear it in his voice?"

"I guess he was just looking out for us. Maybe trying to put a scare into us. Hell, my whole entire life somebody's been trying to put a scare in me one way or the other. It usually don't amount to a warm piss on a cold day."

She shook her head. "It's not what he said. It's how he said it."

"How did he say it?"

"It was a warning, Gus. A warning loud and clear. Directed right at your heart."

I had occasion to think about what she said during the next few weeks.

On June 29, Llewellyn and Hazen met with Doc inside his camp, surrounded by pony boys, and started to work their conspiracy of lies.

That same week, Black Hank—Frank Slaven—was sentenced to jail.

July 1, Trudy and I found Dill Schiller hanged over the Frog Hollow outside Pleasant Valley.

A few days later, Jack Nolan went to jail after trying to rob a post office in Ainsworth.

Not long afterwards, Grimes was shotgunned in two by one of Llewellyn's cohorts, and Chet Tanner vanished from the face of the Earth.

The truth of it was, Trudy was right.

Things were falling apart fast.

Chapter Eighteen

July 19

At Pleasant Valley, on the day Albert returned, I was up before first gray light, fixing on the outside corral. The gate didn't hang right since Jack and Curley ran off with the Pine Ridge remuda, and the bottom rails on the south fence were overgrown with Creeping Jenny and half rotten. The whole place was a mess, and it's not because Trudy wasn't trying. Some things go to hell no matter what. But I was working on a knack for repair.

Puttering around the place had been a tonic to me. Working outside at my own pace gave me the time and space to think. Bringing things in line showed me a side of life I craved but never knew it. Order, organization. God help me—tidiness—and nobody ever would have said it about me.

"You need to think about what kind of man you want to be, Gus."

Fence work gave me time to think about the rivers—their long flow across the landscape. The landscape of history, too. The Keya Paha moved like a garter snake, slipping off wherever it wanted, coursing around curves, sneaking down to the Running Water. And the mighty Niobrara, a rattler crashing through brambles and burdock, crumbling its own banks over time—taking on a new face for each new generation.

Nothing stayed the same.

I couldn't get the ghastly face of Dill Schiller out of my head, hanging there, bloated black and tied off by a noose.

Vigilance committees were nothing new. Every now and then

some old boys would drink too much, get a rage on, and run out after somebody. In the unorganized territories, lynching a horse thief was just a part of life. But organized lynching—methodical and deliberate—was something else again.

A man takes his girl for a walk to the frog pond, he expects to get a mosquito bite. He doesn't expect to be smacked in the face by the sight of an old friend dangling by the neck from a cottonwood bough.

Trudy and I cut Dill down and carried him back to Pleasant Valley, where we buried him behind the house.

The Three-*S* Rule—shoot, shovel, and shut-up. But in this case, we only had to do the last two. Somebody else provided the killing, free of charge.

Albert rode up in the misty rain on a fresh-seeming strawberry roan gelding with a distinctive speckled hide. Beautiful, but easy to identify. It was unlike him to ride such a conspicuous animal. I was surprised I'd never seen the horse before. Just surprised he would come riding in on it bold as brass in broad daylight. But I was thinking for myself, worried about the detectives and the vigilance committee and Otto Randolph's warning.

Kid Wade never worried about anything.

Isn't it funny how different we were, and why hadn't I ever noticed it before?

He sat there staring at me from the back of his horse like we didn't know each other.

The mist wasn't anything like a real rainstorm, just a miserable drizzle we couldn't escape, coming as it was from all directions, like a drunken fog.

Something my ma always said: high country weather's a mad drunk.

She would know.

Al finally spit out a "Howdy-do," and I dropped the hammer in the mud, which splashed towards him.

He wore a long cream-colored slicker and a dark felt hat, looking for all the world like he was coming from a funeral. He tipped his head back toward the house where a wagon and pair of geldings waited outside. "Clausen is here?"

I confirmed the obvious. "Yes, Clausen is here."

"Trudy still trading guns?"

"Not so much as before."

He took the words like an insult, shaking his head. "I guess the whole world's turned upside down."

"What do you mean, the whole world?"

"I come to ask you down to Morris's Crossing. Doc's got a camp south of there."

"Him and Pood ain't in Atkinson?"

"Him and Pood camp all over. He wants you to come. I'm supposed to bring you."

I bent over and picked up my hammer, turned, and hung it from the fence rail. "I don't think I should go. Got a lot of work needing to get done here."

"It's about the pardon they're going to give Doc."

"I been pondering the news," I told him. "You know it's not true. It's a trick of some kind."

"Doc saw a hand-writ draft of the thing. Llewellyn showed him. Doc's just got to sign the official document to make it legal. Doc wants a few of us there to be witnesses."

Once more, I told him, "You know it's not true."

" 'Course it's not true."

"You tell him?"

"Don't matter what I tell him. Doc's a believer. He thinks it's the way to go. So, I guess it's the way it's gonna go."

"That's it?"

"Isn't that about all there is, August John?"

The way he said it made me think about the end of the world, what Trudy called the rapture, and how one day everything would be all done and finished. Most folks, even good folks, would end up in a lake of eternal fire.

Albert talked about Doc's pardon the exact same way.

Like any way you sliced it, we was all going to burn.

I still ain't much of a Bible reader.

Al said, "They're telling Doc all sorts of lies. They're going to make him a detective. He's going to wear a star on his shirt. He's going to be a national hero. The governor of Nebraska, the president of the United States, and Jesus Christ Almighty's gonna stand in line to shake his hand."

"Then what? He's supposed to help round up the Pony Boys? Doc wouldn't sell us out."

I'd never seen Albert sneer like he did then.

But I'd never heard the gallows in his voice before, either. Today I was there for both.

"Like I say, Doc does whatever he wants."

Which was true for all of us.

I said, "I guess I'm the same way. I do what I want. I'm staying put, right here with Trudy."

"He's asked for you, Gus. You and me and Black George. Doc's camp is at the mouth of Laughing Water creek. We meet up tomorrow night."

I picked up my hammer and dismissed him. "You all have fun."

"We'll meet the detectives then. Maybe go on up to Richardson's place afterwards."

"I got fence to fix."

"Doc's seen the hand-writ pardon. Did I tell you? They still need to type it up all formal."

We weren't going anywhere with the conversation then, so I changed the subject, and pretty soon both of us were marinating in the soupy weather, talking past each other, meaning something different than our words.

I think for the first time in his life, Albert was looking straight in the face of growing up. He'd cut up and made jokes and danced around it so long, he'd convinced himself time stood still for the Pony Boys. He wasn't ever getting old or settling down. I knew because, until I'd spent all this time with Trudy, I sorta figured the same.

But it's not true, you know. Time is like weather and women and a bullet to the heart. It's always moving, following an unpredictable course, until it stops. You gotta grab on tight and go with it sometimes, because if you try too hard to steer, you'll fall and bust your head open. And when it stops, brother! It stops.

I think it's what Doc was doing now. He knew he had no choice but hang on and go where things were taking him.

"You know Dill Schiller is dead," I said. "Hanged. Just like Windy and Boots were hanged by the vigilance committee."

The news was nothing to Al.

"Maybe he done it to himself. He wouldn't be the first one to take the easy way out."

I said, "Lantern Hill burns most nights. Ain't you seen it?"

"I don't pay attention to shit like you do."

He clucked his horse forward and back, impatient now.

Irritated.

"You coming with me, or what?"

I watched Sonny Clausen ride away with a wagon full of wood boxes, then clomped inside with squishy wet boots. Trudy had a towel waiting for me, along with a hot cup of chocolate flavored milk. "Where'd you get the chocolate?"

"Clausen brought it."

"What else did he bring?"

"Nothing."

"What did he buy?"

"All there was."

Her bedroom door was hanging open, and the blankets on the bed were tossed and piled up on top of the mattress. There was nothing under the bed. I had never seen the place so clean and free of clutter. Like a cyclone had paraded through and carried away half.

"I don't understand."

"I'm out. I told Clausen."

"Out of business? You mean, you're not selling anymore?"

"Chocolate? Yes. Guns? No."

It's what I had wanted to hear from her, but now I wasn't so sure. It was so abrupt, for a second I got shaky with worry. "How will you make it? How can you afford to keep the station supplied with goods? Are you sure it's the right thing?" I swear my knees were practically knocking, I was so excited, but nervous.

Trudy pulled her sweater around her shoulders tight. It was her way when she was showing confidence, and it made me think I needed a sweater like hers. Maybe she'd make me one? By golly, she did, about a year later.

"We . . . will make it *together.*"

"I just don't know how a man—"

She shushed my lips with her finger. "What did Albert want?"

"You saw him?"

"You should've invited him inside."

"I did. He wouldn't come."

She seemed to understand his moods better than I did.

Or maybe she saw the river changing course.

Again, she asked, "What did he want?"

"He wants me to ride down to Doc's camp. The detectives will be there tomorrow morning. They're offering Doc a pardon for the soldier boy's murder. They say they want him to be a detective."

"It's a lie."

"I know it and you know it, but Doc wants to believe it. He wants me to be there."

"So he sent Albert to come get you."

"Yes."

"What did you say?"

"I told him *yes.*"

"Did you know Henry Richardson once rode with a string of vigilantes?"

Doc Middleton's voice was little more than a murmur, low and hushed, but there wasn't a reason to be so careful. We were both out in the woods, a far piece away from where Al and George and young Ted stood inside the kitchen. I mean, the windows were open, but Pood was pitching a peach cobbler, and the boys were helpless for grub.

As we talked, we walked toward the river. The Running Water was a continuous, bubbling balm to my ears, and the trees were oppressed with birds.

"Henry Richardson? On a vigilance committee?" I thought Doc was maybe teasing me.

"It's true enough. During his younger days back in Montana. Pood told me some stories. Sounds like the old man is proud of his service."

"He calls it a service?"

Doc shrugged. "Yah. Service to the community, to the law. Ain't a hell of a lot of law out here." He grinned so I could see his gold tooth. "In case you hadn't noticed."

"What does Henry think about the goings on here, along the river? Ted told us some vigilantes paid the family a visit."

"Young Ted's got more stories than peach fuzz. I wouldn't put a lot of stock in what he tells you."

"He said Henry and his wife went away for a while because

of the vigs."

"Naw, they just went to pick up supplies in O'Neill City. Nothing more to it."

I thought about the Richardsons' self-imposed exile as Ted had told it. I had no reason to doubt it. I had no reason to believe a word of it, either.

"So you ain't heard from Henry on the subject of vigs along the Niobrara?"

"Henry and me don't talk overly much. He don't talk to Pood anymore, either." Doc cast a whimsical look over his shoulder. "I'm grateful for the use of the house."

"Albert says you and Pood been living in a tent."

"Me and Pood live all over."

"It's what Albert said."

"I don't think these rabble-rousers you're talking about amount to a hill of beans. These men might imagine themselves to be the law, but they aren't organized. It's nothing more than two or three killers looking for revenge against anybody they believed wronged 'em."

"You got any idea who they are?"

"I might," Doc said, and he told me their names.

I said, "God help us if they ever gain in membership and get organized."

Doc cut loose with a big sigh.

"This ain't no way to live, Gus. I'm ready for it to end."

We stopped beside a black mulberry tree, and Doc took out the makings for a smoke. Through the branches, the Niobrara spread out before us, a vast wide mirror reflecting the dull smoky light on the western horizon, its ripples and eddies picking up the reflection of the crescent moon clearing the far tree line. Standing on the moderate crest, looking down into the current, it flowed through my veins sure as blood. Crazy, but I could feel it washing through my head with all its centuries of beneficiaries: plants, animals, men. Who-knows-what else. Booses and snake-monsters and Indian deer-ladies.

This time in the season the berries were perfectly ripe—the right measure of sweetness and tart. The right balance of soft and chewy. Picking them left a hellacious stain on a man's hands—blotchy and hard to scrub away. Like blood.

Doc shook some tobacco onto the paper and rolled it up tight with his forefinger and thumb. He struck a match on his belt next to his holstered .45.

"These detectives are trying to trick you," I said.

He closed his eyes and exhaled slow, letting the apple-tinged smoke curl out of his nostrils before the final push. "Maybe. Maybe not." He looked down at me with his piercing kind eyes. "It's why I want you there, August John."

"I ain't going by that name anymore, Doc."

"You ain't carrying a gun either."

"We ain't supposed to need one for this go-round, are we?"

Chuckle. "You got me there, pard."

"How about a smoke for me?" I said.

He tossed me the pouch of tobacco, handed me a paper, and I caught it one-handed. When I was ready, he offered me a light from the glowing tip of his own cigarette.

"I know about the stolen cow," he said, a casual observation.

"Which cow?"

"The cow you swindled out of young Ted. Albert says he gifted your Trudy with it."

"Oh, she's *my* Trudy, now?"

"Isn't she?"

I didn't argue with him.

After a few minutes, I said, "What about the cow?"

"It ain't yours."

"It was a trade."

Doc said, "It was Albert's trade. You know what those are

usually worth." He shook his head. "Albert's got a mean streak in him. I guess I don't have to tell you, but I want to say it's getting wider. He don't care who he steals from or who he hurts."

"I can bring the cow back to Ted if you want."

Doc shook his head. "Forget the cow. I seen those drunken-*K* horses you brought in from Herko Koster's." He dropped his smoke and crushed it out in the dirt. "So did Llewellyn."

"Did they recognize the brand?"

Doc's grin was contagious. "I didn't go askin' 'em."

A pair of yellow finches swooped around fighting, perching in the light branches of the tree, plucking mulberries.

I ate a few more myself.

"Llewellyn's gonna try and kill you."

"I don't think so." Doc ate a few mulberries. Spit the seeds out over the bank, arcing them toward the river. "Not this time."

I finished my smoke.

After a while, Doc let out with a big sigh. "It's dark soon," he said. "Let's go on inside. In the morning, we'll congregate with the detectives at my tent on the crick, then proceed back here to sign the papers."

I wasn't sure what I heard in his voice, but it was a long ways from joy.

"We best get a good night's sleep," Doc said.

It was resignation.

Chapter Nineteen

July 20

In the end, we lined up like this: Llewellyn dominant and commandeering on a coal-black mare, Doc Middleton on his Red Buck smelling of saddle soap and bay rum, Albert riding the speckled roan, me on my chestnut, and Hazen, bringing up the rear on a broomtail dun not worth three silver dollars.

Five of us dripping with the same soaking mist, three owlhoots and two lawmen, nobody innocent, all of us guilty of twenty times seven sins, each making out like we had the high moral ground. The air smelled of river rot and something dead in the bushes.

The Laughing Water crick wasn't too awful funny.

My arms were jittery holding the reins, like I was full of bugs or St. Elmo's fire, the way it sometimes dances on the horns of Texas beef on stormy nights. I've done my share of nighthawking—whistling "Annabelle" and singing under my breath to keep the herd steady and calm.

Maybe the tune would work on Albert. He was more jittery than me.

I hummed a few bars.

All morning Al had been elusive and flat eyed, like he'd been up all night drinking without sleep. As soon as I had the thought, damned if he didn't pull a flask from his back pocket, take a nip, then drop his drink into a deep pocket on his cream duster. I wished I had a husky sip myself—though I didn't envy his booze habit. But he was dressed better than me.

We all had on our best, being it was Sunday, but the true reason was Doc wanted to celebrate a new beginning. He wore a thick tweedy coat and ivory-white shirt, string tie, and black felt hat—custom built by a hatmaker in Cheyenne. His trousers had a crease in them—unheard of!—and the boots he wore were spit shined with silver spurs. Around his waist was an ornately tooled leather gunbelt with the .45 he bought from Trudy hanging at his hip and tied down to his thigh.

Al wore the same duster and dark hat as before, but it looked like he'd combed his hair, and for once his upper lip was bleached clean. He carried his double-action .38 in its open-end holster.

Llewellyn wore gray, as he had in Paddock, with a round bowler hat. He carried a carbine he said was "just for show," and Hazen was dressed in polished beige with a Winchester rifle blue-black and just as new.

"Lykins is already up to the house," Llewellyn said. "He'll meet us there."

I had steeled myself for coming face to face with the Dutchman again, and now he wasn't here.

How to confront a man you saw almost killed by your friend and mentor—but who for dumb luck survived. The day out on the range, Lykins was a man I might've killed myself had I been carrying a gun.

Trudy was superstitious about Doc's gun jamming that day. When I told her the story, she said, "There are no accidents, Gus." In her view everything was a deliberate piece in some kind of grand puzzle.

Such hooey spun my head around, so I ignored it. It's still funny his gun jamming like it did.

Lykins not being here right away was a let-down.

Lewellyn turned his horse around at the base of a tall Russian thistle patch until he was facing us.

"Albert Wade and John Augustus. I want to thank you men for being with us today."

Men.

"Governor Nance sees this as an opportunity to turn a corner up here in Niobrara River country. A chance for settlers, ranchmen, and cowboys like yourselves to come together in harmony. You three are certainly doing God's work this fine Sunday morning."

Al snickered at him calling us *cowboys.* I smiled at him calling us *men,* but what else could he say? It was true, and we were.

Llewellyn said, "If you'll all follow me along the trail to the Haptonstall house on Henry Richardson's claim, we'll sign the necessary documents and celebrate our new era of cooperation with a grand breakfast." He made it sound like a meeting of the Masons or a charity ball.

It wasn't good Lykins not being here to ride with us. It left me feeling the need to look over my shoulder or behind every swishing clump of grass.

While Llewellyn cranked his steed around, I walked the chestnut up alongside Albert. I had to be careful because Hazen was right behind me. He cleared his throat, loud to get my attention before I talked to Al, so I gave him a nod.

Hazen was a pug-ugly sort with fleshy jowls and brown teeth. Doc said he'd been a bounder, horse thief, and convict in prison until one day he met the Lord. I figure Hazen wasn't given much of a choice, which is how those come-to-Jesus meetings with the Lord mostly went. Or maybe it was a woman hooked him up to heaven.

Hazen winked at me, this kind of Old Scratch move that to me said, "Watch what we've got planned next." I didn't trust any of them devils, which is what I'd been telling Doc and Albert for more than twelve hours.

I leaned into Al as close as I could without falling out of my saddle. "You seen Lykins?"

"I guess he's up to the house."

"It's what Llewellyn told us, sure—but have you *seen* him? With your own eyes."

"It doesn't matter."

"It might matter a whole good goddamn. Lykins could be anywhere."

"What? Like hiding behind a tree?"

"Anywhere."

"Never mind, Gus."

I'd never seen Al so stoic. What was the word again? The word I used for Doc the night before?

Resigned.

I fell back into line, and we started moving up the cow-trail along a scrubby grass-dappled ridge, up over a hump my gut told me was an Indian burial mound, and down through a couple woodsy groves. Despite the damp air, the crick was dry.

Not as dry as my mouth.

I wondered if Trudy was sitting at her table, miles away, sipping hot coffee from fresh grounds and eggshells, maybe eating one of those pullet eggs. Was she thinking about me?

Llewellyn was trotting ahead quite a ways, more than a hundred feet ahead of me. Doc and Al, second and third in line, urged their horses into a good clip behind him. We had at least a mile to go before we'd see the house. I assumed Ted Roberts would be there with Lykins waiting for us. Doc said Black George and maybe James Church, who they called Black Bill.

Doc had a wide variety of friends. A lot of hangers-on.

Not a distinctive damned name among them, to tell the truth. Black-this and Black-that. I sometimes lost track of who was who and which black-hearted S.O.B. was which.

As we rode along toward Richardson's place, Hazen was a like a locomotive breathing down my neck. His horse snapped a twig under its hoof, and I jumped three inches from my saddle, grabbing at my hip for a non-existent firearm.

I made a deliberate choice not to carry one today.

I planned to go home to Trudy alive.

"Haw-haw-haw-haw," bellowed Hazen, like the loud crackling noise was some joke. "What'sa matter, August John? 'Fraid I'm gonna back-shoot you?"

I wouldn't put it past the scurvy muttonhead, but I didn't say it out loud. I held my tongue. I didn't want to be the dog squatting on Doc's big day. Bad dogs get swatted.

"Y'know, you and Kid Wade get quite a bargain out of all this," Hazen said. "What'cha might call a fringe benefit just for showing up."

I didn't like talking to him, but I wanted to appear friendly. "How do you figure?"

Hazen had ridden up beside me, and we could visit pretty much face to face, though he looked straight ahead, never taking his eyes off Llewellyn, far in the lead.

The grass on the right-hand side of the trail was getting taller. Yellow, dry, and gone to seed under the July sun. Today it wilted heavy with drops of rain. We steered out of the way where it bent over into the path, pushing us closer to the side of the crick.

The trail was getting slick with mud.

Hazen cleared his throat again. "I mean the pardon Doc is getting from the governor. There's no legal mention of your name, of course. But just being here today, you and Kid Wade catch some of the overflow. Almost like a baptism. You stand close by, you'll get splashed with holy water." His voice dripped with sarcasm. "All your sins are forgiven, ya damned rustler."

"Hope you ain't countin' on the same good fortune happening for you."

His snotty smirk fell into his lap, and he faced me with a scowl. "You watch what you say, boy. I've got your life right here in my hand." He held up the Winchester, and I spit off the opposite side of my horse.

"Fall back, Hazen, before you step in a badger hole."

Seemed like he was going to say something. Seemed the type who would have an answer for everything. But, instead of more talk, he slid back into place, and I left him behind.

I was pretty sure he wouldn't shoot me in the back, but my spine tingled, and I couldn't help but flex my shoulders over and over again. I drove the chestnut into a trot along the line of grass, catching up close to Al with Doc just in front of him.

"Hazen's saying we're in the clear because of all this. You and me can carry clean slates after today."

"What of it?"

"I'm just relaying the message."

Albert shrugged, took a sip from his flask. Now he carried it openly in his lap. "Want a snort?" he said.

I did.

I passed.

"Llewellyn's kiting out there quite a ways," I said. "What the hell's his hurry?"

"Maybe he's gotta make water."

"You're saying he's full of piss."

It was the last time I ever heard Albert Wade laugh. Short, clipped at the end, but a genuine laugh.

"It's exactly what I'm saying."

It felt good to make Albert laugh. At least one more time.

We rounded a long, sloping curve, and the right-hand grass was nearly as high as our saddles.

Doc turned his head as if to say something to Albert.

He coughed once.

Then came a clink from inside the grass, and I thought one of the horses threw a shoe or skipped a rock. When it came again, almost parallel now with the Red Buck horse, Doc wheeled around, grabbing at his gun.

"By God, there's something wrong here."

A flicker of movement in the grass, and still I was slow on the uptake.

It's a rabbit, I thought, or maybe a wild turkey.

Again with the metallic click, but, this time, Lykins rose from the grass, a Sharps long gun pressed up against his shoulder, its muzzle pointed at Doc's white collar.

Click. Click. The dirty little Dutchman frantically jerked the trigger, his round red face scrunched up like pie dough, blistering mad. Doc swung his arm up with the Peacemaker, firing twice into the grass, the slugs slapping into the sod at Lykins's feet. It all happened faster than anything ever. We were riding along, laughing, starting to relax; now the air was thick with powder smoke.

Lykins gave up on the defective rifle, pitching it aside to reach for the pistol tucked under his black wool coat. Doc careened away from the path as Lykins blazed away, and all I could think was to push between him and Doc.

Up ahead, Llewellyn's black horse was caught off guard and plunged away from the scene into the creek with Albert pounding dirt after him.

I drove my horse directly into Lykins, knocking him off balance. "You son of a bitch," I said but continuing to call him worse.

But now my liver chestnut was turning around in circles, reeling away from the explosions of gunfire. He chased Lykins along the Laughing Water creek bank as I fought the reins. "Whoa, now. Here, fella."

I saw Llewellyn in the distance, his animal kicking the dust for thunder.

Almost immediately I heard Albert shouting up above, and I struggled to regain the trail.

"Dammit, horse," I said. And up above, Al was shouting with all his might: "Can't run from me, you bastard."

More gunfire, seemingly from every direction.

I rose from the crick in time to see Albert go berserk, as I'd seen him with Heavy Frahm's couch, only this time he funneled all his black powder wrath at one man. He rode like a demon after Llewellyn, his cream duster trailing out behind him, enveloping great gusts of blue smoke. "Come and get it, coward."

His arm was a steel fuselage, his hand a living weapon grafted to the .38-caliber iron. He jabbed the gun forward again and again, not hitting a blessed thing with his load. Fire erupted from his fingertips, twice, three times, four.

Ahead of him by a yard's length, Llewellyn's horse ran flat out beside the creek, Al's slugs hemming him in.

Then, a stroke of luck for the detective. He ran between a pair of cottonwood trees, and Al had to rear back and swing around.

"Aaaauuugghhh!"

His scream of outrage and betrayal still echoes in my head to this day.

It's how we all felt.

Llewellyn was on the move, fast as an antelope, sprinting into nothingness. Al unloaded the remains of his cylinder with a couple impotent pops. I imagined he might turn around then. I thought he'd care enough about me and Doc to see what happened.

He kept riding without looking back.

By the time I got back to Lykins, the Dutchman had gotten away. I made out his path through the thicket but didn't see his scruffy carcass anywhere.

We sure took a lot worse than we gave.

Cursing, I jumped down off my horse, turning on my heel in time to see Doc closing in on Hazen. Both men were moving slow, with gut-wrenching jerks.

Still upright, Doc balanced like a theater clown on one boot, a wet stain blossomed at his beltline, scarlet and round against his white shirt.

Hazen was prostrate on the ground, crab-walking backwards, his new beige suit scuffed and stained with a bloody hand print. The detective held up his muddy red fingers to ward Doc away, and the carbine was loose on the earth beside him. I heard him beg, "By the holy name, Doc, let's not kill each other."

I watched Doc aim the .45.

With nary a twitch, Doc punched a ball of lead through Hazen's lung. The old boy jerked and rolled over, kicking, his mouth opening in silent agony. No different than a pig or rooster or an old, sick, cat. He kicked, and I thought sure he was dead, but turned out he wasn't, because he started crawling away toward the crick.

Let him.

I was more worried about Doc. I ran to him and helped him down to the ground so he wouldn't fall over. His knees buckled like they were made of paper, his hat tumbling down to roll into the grass in the spot where Lykins had been hiding.

"Be—be—betrayed," he said, and I cradled his head in my lap. "The bastards . . . betrayed."

"It was an ambush all right."

Llewellyn had planned it all from the beginning. I felt the heat rise in my face. Felt my breath coming faster than it already was. I started to tremble. The shooting was all over, and *now* I trembled!

I said, "They never meant to give you a pardon. They didn't

mean to take you alive."

Doc wasn't hearing me. "D-did I get him?" he said.

"You got Hazen," I said. "I don't know where Lykins is. Albert went after Llewellyn."

"Hazen got me. G-gut . . ."

Gutshot.

"Yeah, the ornery cuss clipped you all right. But don't you worry, Doc. We'll get help."

Doc's head rolled then, and he closed his eyes, still breathing, but raspy, with flecks of dirt and brushy beard in his mouth and nose. I tried to make him comfortable, then jumped up to find Albert.

I picked up Hazen's abandoned Winchester and bolted along the trail toward the twin cottonwoods Al had veered behind. Llewellyn, the coward who set the ambush into play, was far away, and last I knew of Lykins, he was unhurt but also missing. If either of those two decided to swing back around to finish us, I planned to be ready.

I dove through the brush, whipsaw willow sprigs swiping my face, cutting into my cheeks. Thistles tore at my pant legs, and burrs clung to my cuffs. I ran like a madman, calling for Al, shouting at Lykins, using more awful names than I thought I knew.

There was an ongoing echo in my head as I charged. Gunfire and Albert yelling. Doc, startled and surprised.

"By God, there's something wrong here."

The crash of my boots through the underbrush and the flurry of birds I surprised rising from their treetop homes all joined the rush of sound. But it drifted over empty space, and when I came out on the other side of the woods to see the house on the Richardson claim across the creek, I was alone.

I bent over and lost a quart of bile.

Thank the Lord we didn't have breakfast first.

I straightened up, drug my shirtsleeve across my chin, and saw Pood coming from the house with Ted Roberts behind her. Twice she stumbled, and twice her cousin helped her stand.

They must've heard the gunfire, I thought. "Oh, God, what a horror."

I glanced up at the sky, wondering what Trudy would make of it all.

Because Lykins's gun had misfired. Just like Doc's so long ago.

And both of the men were still alive. It was uncanny and odd like all the weird things Trudy talked about after dark.

With Pood and Ted's help, we got Doc onto the back of his horse, and together the three of us took him to the house. Pood decided we ought to get the doctor from up the river, and Ted said he'd go—which suited me fine.

I was still a shaky mess, but after we made sure Doc was resting well on Ted's feather bed, I wanted to get back outside. Inside the house, the walls closed in airtight.

A few days later, they moved Doc to a hidey-hole tent on Wyman Creek.

Meanwhile, Hazen crawled all the way to Preacher Skinner's tent on the Niobrara, where the old man's wife nursed his bleeding wounds.

Llewellyn kept running south. He didn't stop until he got all the way to Fort Hartstuff.

I went back to Trudy.

And Kid Wade was missing.

Chapter Twenty

July 21

Hunkered down in Pleasant Valley, with crossbeams across the doors, Trudy and me could stay put forever.

With the station provisions on the shelves and the chickens outside, we had enough to lay low for quite a while. The cows were good milkers, and we had guns and ammunition. I oiled up my .41 wheel gun, and Trudy propped a Greener shotgun beside the door.

Or—on the other hand—we thought maybe we should pack up the horses, string the cows behind, and go. Leave the country behind.

But go where?

How far did Llewellyn's reach extend? He was out there somewhere. And who would he come after next?

One thing's for sure, we decided: he wasn't going to let the mess at Laughing Water be his last word on the subject of us Pony Boys.

He would be back for Doc Middleton.

He might try to rope in all of us.

It was an anxious time, and Trudy was dazed when I first tried to describe what happened at the gun battle. At first, she didn't believe a word of it. Then she believed too much, embroidering the story into more than it was.

"And Hazen is killed?" she said. "Did you see it with your own eyes?"

I thought so.

"And what about Albert? He's dead?"

Not as far as I knew.

"What if Hazen killed Albert?"

She kept swinging back and forth like the pendulum of a clock. Repeating what I said but making stuff up on her own.

"You've got some names confused," I told her.

And, as it turned out, nobody was killed outright during the gunfight—though Hazen took a direct bullet to the chest. He died some time later. Or maybe he lived to old age. I really don't know.

And it's the way it would go with the tellings and retellings of the Sunday shootout.

Not only for me and Trudy, but for the whole territory and all the rest of history—what they call posterity.

Doc's legacy was as wide as the frontier, and his name was already famous like Alexander Graham Bell or Napoleon. No matter how a man tries to tell the straight ahead series of events, some nut wants to change it up. He'll put Doc up high as a victim or down low as a black-hat gunslinger. Well, he wore a black hat. God's honest truth.

Nobody ever told the story straight, not even Doc.

Naturally, we didn't know what the future would bring when I came home Sunday night after the ambush. I guess I had some blood spatter on my hands and on my clothes. Trudy tried to help me undress because I was shaking too hard to undo my buttons.

We still hadn't been together—in the way of a husband and wife—so I went out to the barn to change clothes and help Buddy the calf eat his supper. He was half growed up and didn't need me anymore. I slumped down in my stall to hide from the world, eyeing Richardson's cow. It all made me depressed.

Then I moped all the more, thinking about Doc saying he

knew about the cow. The detectives knew about the drunken-*K* horses. My sins were on display to the entire world.

Hazen's voice growled in my ears. *"All your sins are forgiven, ya damned rustler."*

I said, "Not now they're not."

It took me an hour to get the blood scrubbed off my hands, using sand and lye soap.

I guess I had maybe the shortest salvation on record.

I went back inside, and Trudy and me ate 'til we were sick and got drunk on Clausen's rum, and before long I started jumping at my own shadow.

The next day, Monday the 21st of July, 1879, I figured I'd go to work like usual, tending the animals, 'provin' up on the place. What else could I do? And, besides, staying busy took the edge off my rattled nerves.

I carried my hammer back to the outside corral with determination. The pen seemed bigger than ever, the size of all the West. "I'm gonna keep working on the fence," I told myself. "One day it'll be done, or I'll drop dead first." It felt good to work.

I pulled out two rotten rails and cut a couple replacement boards with an old rusty saw. The work was steady, the weather more hot than the day before, the mist and clouds finally breaking up. I stripped off my shirt, and my back started to crisp up sore and red. Glorious.

I planned to bake out my nerves. I'd sweat out Clausen's booze. I'd work honest on the fence, making something to last.

Albert's story about the prairie fire burning Konicek's fence spurred me on. It only made me want my corral to be fit and trim. I skipped lunch and labored on through the afternoon, feeling more steady, more sure of myself.

Somebody had to stand up and do the work. Somebody had to make things right.

If the whole blasted world quit building fences because of one disappointment, we'd be in some sorry damn state. Who would have a right to say anything?

I had high thoughts all day, more proud of my work than ever. Proud of my new commitment.

By the time darkness started to fall, I was almost what you might call relaxed. The previous morning was far away, and when I recalled the gunfire and smoke, I deliberately pushed it from my mind.

I knew Doc was out there hurting. Albert might be in some kind of trouble. But I couldn't feel them anymore. It was like they didn't exist. Like I'd imagined them in my own feverish dreams.

I told Trudy about how I felt the first time I rode into Pleasant Valley, about how I felt all alone, like a tiny speck of life in a vast unorganized range. It's the way I felt again, but now the two of us were together, and we were working to build a life together. We had a foundation called Pleasant Valley.

I was so busy gathering wool, I wasn't ready when the vigilance committee came.

Damn sheepherder.

The sun had just dropped behind the tall hill to the west when I saw the light on Lantern Hill. They fired it up fairly regular now, and all I could do was keep my head down and look ahead at my new life, playing it straight as a station manager and merchant. I'd raise a few calves; we'd keep the chickens.

Trudy said it was time to bring the "pleasant" back to Pleasant Valley.

The column of dust clouds, like Indian smoke writing, marred the orange and pink haze of the horizon, and a pounding roll of horses' hooves came to me at the corral. Trudy had just carried out a cup of coffee for me, and we watched them come in together.

There were three of them, all black horses with gleaming manes and tails of wild energy, the moon glinting silver against them. They snorted and blowed, chuffed and pinned back their ears. Their eyes rolled in their heads, and the men atop their backs barely kept them constrained.

I told Trudy to get to the barn and hide.

I ran for the house and my .41-caliber pistol.

One of the dark riders cut me off, scrambling between me and the front door. The other two horses fell in behind me.

"Hold fast, John Augustus," said the vig in front of me. He wore a black cloth mask with holes cut for his eyes, and the hat on his head was a tall felt Stetson. Around his neck was a string tie holding a long cloak, and his pants were tough and stained dark as night.

All the men were dressed the same, like the night.

I marched right up to the man, demanding an explanation.

"What the hell's the meaning of this?"

He hit me with a coil of rope. "Shut up."

I stumbled backwards, almost fell. But I stayed upright. To this day I'm proud of holding my own. The sumbuck was surprised. I didn't need to see his face to know it. His next sentence conveyed the tone. I don't think a lot of people stood up to them.

"Tough little runt are you?"

"I get by."

One of the men behind rode up and tried to plant a boot on the back of my skull.

I slipped sideways, lashed out, and managed to tear a fingernail on the black steed's leather tack. But nothing else. I stuck the finger in my mouth—it hurt like a house a'fire.

"Careful, Gus," said the leader man. Something about the way he talked was fake. Like he was deliberately changing the timbre so's I wouldn't recognize him. In the dusk, I tried to peg him by his body shape, but the damned cloak covered a multitude of sins.

Of course Doc had already told me who he was, and, with that knowledge, it was easy to see through the theatrics.

"I'm disappointed in you, Otto Randolph. You've sat in our store and drunk our coffee. I thought you were my friend."

Randolph chuckled under his hood. "Ain't no such man as Otto Randolph here tonight, Gus. Tonight, I'm the Law. And it's the Law you need to answer to. You and your wench, both."

I was already mad as a hornet stuck in honey but damned if I would stand there and let him call Trudy names.

With Randolph taking the lead, the men started walking their horses around in a circle, meaning to taunt me and get me dizzy. The night before, on the heels of Doc's shoot-out, I might've fallen over with exhaustion and lost everything I thought I still had. But not tonight.

"Are you the men who hanged Windy Barnes and Boots Harper? What about Dill Schiller? Those men were friends of mine."

"So you admit being in league with the scum plaguing our good homes?"

"I admit to having friends. Do you admit to killing them?"

"They were executed, son. As they deserved."

One of the other men wasn't so coy. His pride couldn't be contained. He just had to share the accomplishment. "Damn right we did it."

Randolph kept rambling on—like he was on stage, reciting lines somebody else wrote for him.

"You're as much scum as they were, August John. More so because you don't limit your dealings to Indian horseflesh. The only thing left for you is justice—swift and without mercy. It comes for all horse thieves."

Round and round in circles they went around me. And there I was, standing stock-still, not letting the motion throw me off balance, not trying to keep up with Randolph's black horse, but continuing to chatter, to match him word for word and find the salt-of-the-earth rancher I knew lived underneath the costume.

"You're a good man, Randolph. You oughtn't kill folks without a fair shake."

"You and Kid Wade prey on your good neighbors. Do they get a fair shake?"

The dirty dog. I'd set him straight. "You're wrong. I never intentionally went after my neighbors. I've lived here most of the summer. I am a good neighbor."

"I'm sick of your lying mouth, Gus." Randolph motioned to one of the others, then he waved at the barn. "Go get Richardson's cow."

The horseman obeyed the request, trotting over to the barn's open alleyway. Again, I talked direct to Randolph.

"What's this about a cow?"

"You deny you're keeping Henry Richardson's cow?"

"Albert and I swapped young Ted for it."

"Young Ted can't swap lunch with a coon dog. You stole it outright. Tried to hide it over here. You ain't such a good neighbor after all."

"How do you know so much?"

"It's our goddamn job to know," said Randolph. He held his coil of rope out at arm's length and unraveled a plentiful length. "I saw the brand the other day when I was leaving. Hell, I tried to give you a friendly warning. But then I came outside, and there she was in the barn."

"Why were you snooping in my barn?"

"You're in no position to judge me."

"Here's your cow," said the man over by the barn. I could see he had Henry's cow on a lead.

"Now you'll make restitution, boy." Randolph dropped the loop of his rope over me quick as a cat scratch, and I lurched to the side, doing my best to yank him out of the saddle. The hemp bit through the material of my shirt, scraping against my sunburn, digging into my arms and back.

Randolph's black horse moved forward a few steps, and the vig jerked the rope tight, cinching my arms to my side, squeezing the air from my guts. I felt cut in two.

I couldn't breathe.

Another loop fell over my head with a hard thud.

I wriggled like crazy, trying to get the rope to drop over my shoulders, but this one closed under my chin, tore into my neck. Squeezing.

Randolph's voice was tough, without any kind of sentiment. He was out of his skull with the power of life and death. "You got any last words, runt?"

I let all my torso weight fall against the first rope in a desperate, loco attempt to unseat Randolph from his saddle. It almost worked. Again the horse took a few inadvertent steps, and we posed together only a few feet from the front door of the station.

Randolph tugged both ropes, wrenching me off my feet. I smacked hard onto the side, my open jaw catching a mouthful of dust.

The station door opened.

Trudy stepped out with the Greener shotgun, jerked the trigger, and tore a hole the size of Old Baldy out of Randolph's guts.

Above me, the black horse went madly to the right as its rider tumbled left.

Randolph was dead before he crashed into the ground.

As I fell, the other rope would've broke my neck had the second vig not taken Trudy's next shot of buckshot to the face.

He dropped the rope and fell off his animal backwards.

The instant the rope went slack, I rolled with it. All I could think was the last vig might start blasting away at any second out of desperation. I tensed up against the impact of the slugs, but no explosions came.

In a flash of moonlight, I saw Trudy drop the scatter gun and lift my pistol toward the sky.

She was a better shot than Albert Wade. More calm. More ruthless.

One last bullet to the head, and the third man crumpled. The immediate threat was past.

I stripped the ropes from my body and enjoyed a long, loving embrace from Trudy.

Afterwards, I went to find the shovel.

July 27

The next week Llewellyn came back from Fort Hartstuff with soldiers and enough firepower to wipe out the Confederate army, and I finished the corral on the same day. I was so proud of it, I could've bust.

Clausen had taken a shine to my work, too, and I welcomed the old freighter's advice.

He could always get good deals on metal fixtures and tools and such. I made a nice head latch with vertical upright stanchions and an iron lever to slide the lock in place, and I made a squeeze chute and added a gate with iron hinges. I figured on working cows after we raised up a herd from Buddy and Henry Richardson's cow.

Anyway, the old man helped me mount the gates, and Trudy paid him off with chocolate pie and whipped cream. If he noticed the three fresh mounds of dirt behind the house, he was smart enough to keep his mouth shut.

Clausen rode out just before sunset, ten minutes before Kid Wade rode in, looking beat for a dog, his clothes in a shambles.

I was still outside when Al reined in, and I met him in front of the barn.

For this visit, Al didn't want to talk from on high. He slid off his horse's bare back, and I grabbed for his arm. His greeting of four words made me suck wind. "They took Doc away."

It was over then.

I let him put his arm around my shoulder for support, and we walked toward an overturned pail, where he sat. I leaned against the open doorframe of the barn, the sweet smell of cows and hay and dusty grain filling my nose.

Albert smelled like powder smoke and cigarettes.

I'm not sure why, but I didn't want Al inside the house with Trudy. He wasn't wearing his gun, and his face was cloudy with sorrow. There was no reason not to extend him all the hospitality we had before.

Except, somewhere along the line, I'd decided Albert was a bad man.

We were no longer saddle-pards.

He wasn't funny, not even a little bit, and his antics were self absorbed and stale. He was mean spirited and sharp tongued, and he lied more than anybody I ever knew.

Like a snapping turtle or a scorpion, I trusted him only to be himself.

And I didn't like him.

"What happened?" I said.

"Llewellyn came back with reinforcements. Doc and Pood have been camping in a hidey-hole down at Wyman Crick. Nobody knew where exactly except me and the Richardsons. Black Bill knew. We've been carrying water for them, bringing food from Henry's house."

"I sure am relieved to know Doc's alive," I said.

"Hazen is alive, too. Preacher Skinner and a doctor friend of his have been looking out for him."

"I thank you for bringing the news. We've been worried."

"We?" Albert's head jerked up, nervous, paranoid, like I'd said a surprise. Then he looked past me, understood I was including Trudy in my talk, and he put his face back into his hands. "Sure . . . sure."

"Can I get you some coffee, Al?"

"No, nothing for me." He ran his palm up and down his face. "I'll be sick if I eat or drink anything."

"You need to keep up your strength," I said, sounding crazy, acting like a parent.

"The crazy thing is, Doc was doing better, you know? Another few days he would've been good to ride. We had a chance, Gus. We could've . . ." He didn't finish his sentence, and I didn't want to push him. *Could've what? Escaped? To where?*

One wrong word and he'd go off on me like he did on Heavy's daybed, or when he chased Llewellyn through the trees.

He was showing all the signs, but, like I said, he wasn't carrying his gun. I wondered if he lost it. It would be worse if he hit me with his fists.

Finally, he said, "The hell with it."

"How did Llewellyn find you?"

Al said, "The detectives took over Richardson's place. They sweated thunder out of Henry and Ted." His voice was strained but still defiant.

Angry.

"When they came to Doc's camp, they unloaded with rifles into the tent. They had no intention of taking anybody alive. Just like before. They could've killed all of us."

"You were in the camp?"

Al nodded. "Yeah, me and Bill were in the tent with Doc and Pood. They tore hell out of the thing. We lived through a goddamn blizzard of lead. A miracle if there ever was."

"Llewellyn took Doc?"

"They took him all right. Bound up like a wild animal. I got away and made it to the far hills." He nodded. "Then I came here. I guess they weren't after us this go 'round."

"What next?"

"What next? What do you mean—what next?"

"It's the end of things," I said. "The end of Doc, the end of the Pony Boys."

"You and me are Pony Boys," he said. "You said it before."

Above us, the stars were coming out, popping to life with their warm, tranquil glow.

After a while Albert said, "You and me will rest up here a few days, then we'll get back to the trail. What do you say we forget about Pine Ridge? Let Little Wound cool down? We could make a run on Spotted Tail's horses at the Rosebud. What do you think about it?"

I shook my head. "Not me, Albert. I'm out."

"Out? The hell."

"I mean it, I'm out."

"Not with me, you ain't. Nobody's out until I say so. Doc ain't here now." He got all lathered up then, like his coat was full of possums all hissing and clawing. "I can do what I want. Far as anybody is concerned, I'm god of this whole damn river country. What I say, goes."

I didn't disagree with him. His blood churned because of his bad day, and I knew it. But I needed to make myself clear. "I have to stay with Trudy."

"She don't need you. She's got her guns. She's got Clausen."

"She quit with the guns. We're making an honest go of things, Al."

He chewed on it a few minutes, then curled his upper lip and started down a wrong-headed line of thought. "You ain't part of all this, are you, Gus?"

"I don't know what you mean."

"Black Bill says them stock detectives sweated out the Richardsons, but I guess it might've been you betrayed us just as soon as anybody."

I guess my feelings were a little bit hurt by the accusation, but I wasn't surprised.

Al said, "You knew where Doc was hiding all along, didn't you? Have you been talking to Llewellyn?"

"It wasn't me, Al."

"Yeah. Yeah, now I think about it—it makes sense. You never wanted to come with me the last time. I had to beg your ass to come be there for Doc."

"Here now," I said. "You know it's not true."

"No, it is true. I just now remembered it." He stood up with a violent, rough start and kicked the pail across the yard with a bang. "You dirty skunk. It was you all the time. How long have you been working against me? Since the day Windy and Boots took those notch-ears? Since before Doc's wedding?"

Knowing it wouldn't do any good to talk back to him, I held my tongue.

"It's why you wanted to get out of Humpy's so quick that day out in Paddock. You didn't want me to hear one of those law boys making love to you. You got us out of there before somebody slipped up and clued me in on the plan."

"There was no plan. I was as much in the dark as you."

Al spat at my feet and stomped off toward his horse. "You rotten backstabber."

"Albert . . ."

"We're through, August John. I told you before—one more chance. But no more. You and me are quits."

"Albert . . . Kid . . . wait."

He turned around, and, just for a fleeting second, I saw my

old friend in his expression. I saw the day back in April, running horses from Pine Ridge, Albert with his heels pulled up to his gelding's withers and arms outstretched.

"Lookee me—I kin fly."

The silly sumbitch.

He never could fly.

He never would.

And then he turned away, mounted his horse, and was gone.

Chapter Twenty-One

After Llewellyn took Doc into custody, they carried him by stage to Columbus and on to Cheyenne for trial. He healed up from his injury, and they chucked him into the Nebraska pen. One day, a few years later, he got out and left our part of the country behind.

I guess he had just about enough of us pony boys to last a lifetime. I talked to him once more before he died, but I guess that's another story.

Frank Weigand was the constable of the Eastern Precinct of Knox County in those days, a man I never met but heard plenty about—a tough customer. A few weeks after Albert left Pleasant Valley, Frank cornered him on the Weigand farm, arresting him for the theft of Herko Koster's horses—those damned drunken-*K* animals what caused me no end of hurt—but I got the grulla back from Ted Roberts about a month later.

She was a good old horse, and I got to keep the cow.

In the fall, Weigand and his boys put on a show with Al in Niobrara City. The great horse rustler, Kid Wade, was a spectacle, and they made him do some tricks with his lariat rope. Al was always a fine roper. "Look how we're cleaning things up in river country," they said. "First Doc Middleton captured and now the Kid in custody."

Well the Niobrara jail couldn't hold ol' Slippery Jack for long, and they knew it. Woodbury County wanted him just as bad across the Missouri River because of taking the horse from old man Leonard in Iowa. So they took Albert on to Sioux City and tried him in October. I would have liked to go, but by the time I heard about it, the trial was already over.

Sonny Clausen was there, and he told me all about it during one of his rum deliveries.

"Your old pal was miserable mean," he admitted under his breath so Trudy wouldn't hear. "Acting out and cutting up. He jumped over a table and scattered papers around, warning the jury he would make things hot for them if he was convicted and ever got free."

The direction Al went, I said it didn't surprise me.

Clausen said, "The Kid's got old Herko Koster on a vendetta list should he ever be released. He named you and Trudy, too."

"I wouldn't know why."

"He said he would make things hot for everybody who betrayed him."

It's the way he had started thinking.

They sentenced Albert to three years in the Iowa State Reformatory in Anomosa, and he served from November, 1879, until June 7, 1882.

Those years saw hard winters for the Niobrara rough country and lots of immigration from all over the world.

Pleasant Valley station grew, and Trudy and I were pledged together forever.

We had a good home with Betty and Buddy and our worthless dog, Moses McGee.

And then sometime in the summer of '83, horses started disappearing along the Keya Paha. Just a few at first but then more and more—a definite trend.

Some people said it was booses, and some said Dáxte-Wáu—the Sioux Indian deer-lady.

But I knew better. At night there was a light burning on Lantern Hill, and I remembered what I said to Doc about God help us if them vigs ever get organized.

A long time ago, on a starlit night, Kid Wade told me we were quits.

Of course, he never did keep his word.

AUTHOR'S NOTE

I was seventeen years old in 1983, living beside the Niobrara rough country if not actually in it, more than a century after Albert "Kid" Wade and his Pony Boy cohorts roamed the unorganized territories west of Holt County, stealing horses, raising hell, and generally having the time of their lives. More than once, I saw his ghost in the guys I ran with. More than anything, I wished I could've met them.

Doc Middleton, Kid Wade, Curley Grimes and Jack Nolan, Black George and Black Bill and Black Hank, Limber Dick, and Count Shevaloff—these fellow Nebraskans from history lived and breathed the Keya Paha air on the chronological edge of a new era of law and order. They were the last of a passing vocation, all but forgotten by the time I took the high-country stage.

Forgotten by the teachers in my high school who never mentioned them. Forgotten by my grandparents and great-grandparents, who surely heard of their exploits but didn't find them interesting enough to mention. But never forgotten by the adventure motorcyclist Danny Liska or his Native American friends along the Running Water.

Decades before Danny was born on the Liska ranch, it was the Bozik place, and Kid Wade worked there as a hired hand and at the farm next door. Among the Niobrara natives, stories like Kid Wade's fence—related here as I heard it first from Danny—were still shared. Legends were still hotly debated by old men over steaming cups of coffee.

What was the real relationship between Doc Middleton and the Kid? How did Henry Richardson view Doc tying the knot with his daughter? What was William H. H. Lewellyn's true intent for Doc, and what were the play-by-play logistics of the Laughing Water shootout between them?

A good many of the characters and events in this novel are real. Specific details and character traits relating to them come solely from my imagination. Many characters, including August John, Trudy Haas, Otto Randolph, Sonny Clausen, Heavy Frahm, the hanged boys, and the Cernek family, are of my own invention or come from amalgamations of historic people.

There were indeed vigilantes on the rise in those days, and Oglala Sioux Chief Little Wound spurred action against the horse thieves' incursions onto agency lands. From the first chapter of this novel on, the Pony Boys' days were numbered.

What could it have been like to ride with the Kid? To look to Middleton as a mentor? How would I find my way in such a world? These are some of the questions I asked as I approached my research—at first a study of memories from late-night visits thirty years past when stories about the booses and Dáxte-Wáu flowed like the hot coffee we shared and, later, from the following sources.

Danny's colorful anthology, *Bigfoot 7* (1987), containing my own first published work. *Doc Middleton, The Unwickedest Outlaw* by John Carson (1966). "The Lynching of Kid Wade" by T. Josephine Haugen, *Nebraska History Magazine*, January–March, 1933. "On the Hunt for Doc Middleton" by Alan J. Bartels, *Nebraska Life*, May–June, 2011, and the history columns of Ellen Tobin from the *Yankton Press and Dakotan.*

To these I'm forever grateful.

Finally, there are not enough superlatives to describe the studious work, clear writing, and fine attention to detail by

Harold Hutton, the bedrock foundation for any discussion of Doc or the Kid. Just as I'll always cherish my friendship with Danny Liska, I'm indebted to Hutton's books, *Vigilante Days: Frontier Justice Along the Niobrara,* The Swallow Press, Incorporated, 1978, and *The Luckiest Outlaw: The Life and Legends of Doc Middleton,* University of Nebraska Press, 1992.

August John's story is far from over, and Kid Wade's return to the region—this time as a gang leader in his own right—has yet to be shared. The Pony Boys' time is long past, but their legacy is only beginning to be explored.

Richard Prosch
Somewhere South of the Niobrara River

ABOUT THE AUTHOR

Richard Prosch grew up planting corn, tending cattle, and riding the Nebraska range in a beat-up pickup and a '74 Camaro.

With his wife he developed licensing style guides for several cartoon properties and worked with Tribune Media Services and the Hallmark Channel. In the 2000s, Richard built a web development studio while winning awards for illustration and writing (including a Spur Award from the Western Writers of America). His work has appeared in novels, numerous anthologies, *True West, Wild West, Roundup,* and *Saddlebag Dispatches* magazines, and online at *Boys' Life.*

Richard lives on a Missouri acreage with his wife, Gina, son, Wyatt, and an odd assortment of barn cats.

The employees of Five Star Publishing hope you have enjoyed this book.

Our Five Star novels explore little-known chapters from America's history, stories told from unique perspectives that will entertain a broad range of readers.

Other Five Star books are available at your local library, bookstore, all major book distributors, and directly from Five Star/Gale.

Connect with Five Star Publishing

Website:
gale.com/five-star

Facebook:
facebook.com/FiveStarCengage

Twitter:
twitter.com/FiveStarCengage

Email:
FiveStar@cengage.com

For information about titles and placing orders:
(800) 223-1244
gale.orders@cengage.com

To share your comments, write to us:
Five Star Publishing
Attn: Publisher
10 Water St., Suite 310
Waterville, ME 04901